ELFIE

SEASON 3

GABRIELLE DUBOIS

Translated from the French by
Marybeth Timmermann

CONTENTS

ELFIE

SEASON 3

GABRIELLE DUBOIS

EPISODE 1

The Lantern and the Legion of Honor Medal

Angus King's latest play was set to be produced in Paris in June of 1866. So in May, the author and his alibi returned to France.

Despite the fact that Lord Wanton had warned them to no longer frequent the Dorléac, a week after their arrival, they were both invited to a masquerade ball at Marina d'Orléac-Howard's mansion on Courcelles Street.

One man stood out like a sore thumb among the sumptuous evening dresses with appealingly low necklines adorned with the most brilliant jewels and the men's black frock coats worn over impeccable white vests. As part of his costume, this man wore an old, threadbare, long coat made of soft green velvet. As if he were on the village square, he did not remove his frayed, wide-brimmed hat that covered his forehead and hid his eyes. Upon his stooped back, attached by leather straps and held in place on a wooden plank, he carried a box. This guest was disguised as a magic lantern showman.

Without a word, he placed his burden on a stand and invited the men to look into his lantern. One by one, they leaned over and pulled off their masks to put their eye up to the glass lens. When they left, they smiled knowingly or laughed outright with conspiratorial satisfaction.

Angus also looked into the lantern, and had the same reaction afterwards. Elfie was curious and glanced at him questioningly.

"Does the young lady want to take a quick look?" asked the man.

"Angus?" she asked.

"Do as you wish, Elfie."

She had seen a magic lantern before, when she was a little girl, with her mother in Clamart. It showed funny little animated scenes of disobedient children feeling sorry for their mistakes, or a little morality lesson about family life meant to edify the mothers as much as their children.

"Before looking in, mademoiselle," said the man dressed up as a magic lantern showman pedantically, "you must say the magic words."

"What are they?" asked Elfie, amused at his formality.

"The magic words are, 'Thank you, sir, for showing me this scene, and I promise in the future to follow its advice!'"

"Thank you, sir," said Elfie with a smile, "for showing me this scene, and I promise in the future to follow its advice!"

Then Elfie leaned over and peered into the lantern through the glass lens.

The scene was bucolic; a cute shepherdess from the preceding century was wearing a short skirt and frolicking in a prairie, surrounded by two or three white, woolly sheep. A marquis, wigged and powdered as in the olden days, came in and caressed the pretty girl's cheek, hiked up her skirt and then, exposing his own family jewels, went back and forth in thrusting movements to the rhythm of the images.

Elfie jumped and quickly stepped back, her cheeks and temples bright red. All around, the men couldn't stop laughing. Elfie flushed again as she remembered the magic words she had said before looking into the lantern.

"But I thought magic lanterns only showed morality lessons for children!" she explained.

"It is a morality lesson," one of the guests assured her. "But a morality lesson for adults. Personally, I follow it every day!"

"As always," said the lantern showman, setting off a new wave of laughter, "the ones who do it the least are the ones who talk about it the most!"

Angus placed his arm on Elfie's bare arm.

"On the contrary, the young lady rarely speaks of it."

"Yes, I rarely ever speak of it," she exclaimed, confused, realizing too late what she implied by saying that.

"How lucky you are, King!" exclaimed the lantern showman.

Yes, for many, Miss Montesquiou was that charming young lady who had cured Mr. King of his deviant penchants.

It's not important, thought Elfie, who loved her life with Angus. Who cares what they thought or said behind her back— she was having a lot of fun. Whatever the future held, she was living a life that was infinitely more worthwhile than the one she would have been living if she had become Mrs. d'Orvigny.

And on this particular evening, they had not yet finished laughing...

Angus introduced Elfie to the wife of Emile de Chabanais, the creator of the *Free Thought?* newspaper.

"Why is there a question mark at the end of the title?" Elfie had asked Angus the first time she had seen the newspaper the previous year, not long after she had left her home.

"Chabanais could have called his newspaper *Free Thought* without the question mark, but that would have been a lie. Everything that is written in the newspapers must be approved by the censors before being published. And Chabanais is an honest man. So he added this question mark so as not to dupe his readers and so that every week he can make fun of the censors, who have never even wondered why there is a question mark."

Aurore de Chabanais wrote short stories under the pseudonym Baron de Vernaize. Just like her husband Emile, she professed equality between men and women. That evening, on Courcelles Street, she had a lengthy discussion with Elfie and asked her to tell the whole story of how she ended up as Mr. King's companion. Without revealing the exact nature of her relationship with Angus, Elfie recounted the circumstances that had led her to run away from home.

"It is intolerable that a woman be reduced to marry a man she does not want anything to do with!" raged Aurore. "It incenses me when a woman is forced into a marriage of her father's choosing, when his only aim is to further his social position, or of her husband's choosing, when his only concern is his financial ambition."

Never before had Elfie heard such a declaration. Up until then, she thought she was the only woman struggling with her life choices. *I thank you and love you!* she wanted to shout to Aurore de Chabanais, but she didn't dare and smiled at her gratefully.

"Despite what you say, ma'am— and your words bring me more comfort than you can imagine— I am not yet sure of having made the right choice by leaving my home. This life..."

"It's not the life you had imagined, is it?" asked Aurore de Chabanais gently.

"Not really. Oh, I'm not complaining at all!" insisted Elfie. "Mr. King and I get along very well."

"And I am happy for you. But we still have a long way to go before a woman will be able to take charge of her own life on an equal footing with a man."

Elfie started to laugh.

"A woman, the equal of a man? That's not possible! Men know..."

Mrs. de Chabanais smiled and cut her off.

"We might not live to see it, but it will happen, mademoiselle, I am sure of it. Young women such as yourself, fleeing from prostitution, set an example for future generations."

Besides not fully grasping the meaning of Aurore's statement, Elfie was shocked by the word.

"Please excuse me," continued Mrs. de Chabanais. "The moment I sense a receptive audience, I have a tendency to get fired up. Let me explain myself. Do you know the meaning of that word?"

"Yes, I think so," Elfie admitted timidly.

"What is the difference, do you think, between a woman like that and a teenage girl who is given by her father to the man of his choice in order to fulfill his personal ambitions? What would you call the status of a wife, dependent upon her husband for living expenses, and bound to fulfill her conjugal duty?"

"I've never looked at it from that perspective."

Aurore de Chabanais gave Elfie a moment to digest this theory.

"What does your husband think of this, ma'am?" whispered Elfie in alarm. "Does he know what you believe?"

"Emile's beliefs are even more extreme on the subject. That's why I married him."

"Are there other men like your husband, ma'am?"

"Ah, ah! Very few, I think. But you'll find one. I hope you do."

What a brilliant woman this Mrs. de Chabanais is, thought Elfie. To show herself worthy, she confided:

"I am trying to earn enough money to pay for my own expenses. I write. I don't make enough money yet, but I hope to."

"Keep it up, mademoiselle. I hope you succeed."

"I have heard ladies say that if married women had the right to work outside the home, they would win their freedom. Do you believe that?"

"No, I don't think that women working outside the home is the solution. Which women do you mean? Women who have never worked a day in their life besides arranging flower bouquets or practicing the piano? If a woman wants and is able to live off her writing, her painting, or any other work she desires, then more power to her— a self-chosen work is gratifying. But what sort of work do you think the majority of women would do? Factory workers, laundresses, housemaids? These are exhausting, mind-numbing jobs. And who, in your opinion, will raise their children while they work at the factory? Their husbands who also work, or who, if they don't work, won't in a million years want to cook meals and do the laundry? It's not through the workplace that women will win their freedom, but instead would lose what little they have, in my opinion. A paid job would only be an additional task for them, and an even heavier burden that would be piled upon all the other work women already do."

"What can be done, then?" asked Elfie who was hanging on every one of Aurore's words.

"Revisit the mentalities and the laws in order to force men to consider women as their equals. Just because a man is the breadwinner for the household doesn't mean he is the only one with rights. If he thinks that, then he should marry no one and do his own shopping, cleaning, and cooking. All those tasks that women do are not owed to men, but an exchange between two adults who respect each other's work. If a man wants to have a loving wife and children who will make him happy and carry on his name, then he must learn how to appreciate their true value..."

The two women turned around, their conversation interrupted by a slight commotion...

One of the guests was a Mrs. Choiseul, wife of the famous musician and a charming person with a mischievous look in her eyes, a little turned-up nose, and bright, attractive lips. Although she was in her thirties, she retained an enviable youthfulness. All throughout the evening, she had been making eyes at Secretary Rouher. Just past midnight, she was seen slipping into an upstairs bedroom reserved for ladies to reapply their powder or adjust their stockings.

When she reappeared, one might have sworn that she had taken an hour-long hike through the countryside. She looked so alive and provocative; her skin was flushed and her heart was heaving beneath her too-tight corset. Head held high, she was crossing the drawing room as Mr.

Rouher in turn entered from the direction of that same staircase.

Mrs. Choiseul made her way through the crowd with dignity, but behind her, people were unable to stifle their laughter, which erupted in her wake. It took a helpful friend to take her aside and point out to her that Secretary Rouhar's Legion of Honor medal was stuck to the lace on the back of her skirt. No one had any more doubts as to what happened between those two, whose gymnastic talents were witnessed only by the upstairs bedroom!

Neither Aurore de Chabanais nor Elfie could hold back their laughter.

Then Marina d'Orléac-Howard asked Elfie to sing. This risqué evening reminded the former boarding school girl of a song that Francine had recently taught her at Rue de Morny:

"Sidonie has more than one lover
That is a well-known fact
She admits with a sense of pride
Sidonie has more than one lover
Because for her, no clothes at all
Is the most charming garment of all
That is a well-known fact
Sidonie has more than one lover
She catches them with her long blond hair
Like a spider in her web ensnares
Catches the hornets and the flies
Catches them with her long blond hair
Drawn toward her sun-lit eyes
They fly, these poor butterflies
Like a spider with her web ensnares
She catches them with her long blond hair

*She leads them by the nose
Like a rattlesnake does so well
To silly birds fallen under its spell
She leads them by the nose
When from her pout she reaches out
Her tongue with shocking speed
Like the rattlesnake who needs to feed
By her charm she does mislead
She catches them with her teeth
When laughter opens her mouth
And devours the unwary louts
She catches them with her teeth
Her mouth when she goes to sleep
Stays pink with her teeth tucked inside
But when laughter opens her mouth
She catches them with her teeth
Sidonie has more than one lover
Whether you scold her, or give her praise
She's gonna laugh at you either way
Sidonie has more than one lover
And until one of these days
When she's nailed in her pinewood grave
Whether you scold her, or give her praise
Sidonie will have more than one lover."*

While she was standing near the piano singing, Elfie noticed that François-Xavier Howard, Mariana's son, who had just arrived, approached Angus King and was whispering into his ear. Angus seemed irritated and eventually moved away. From time to time, Howard shot a nasty look toward the singer. Even from so far away, his resentment was palpable. Elfie could sense the deviousness emanating from Howard, just as she had on the first day she had ever met him in Violette Roi's drawing room.

In the hansom cab taking them back to Rue de Morny, Elfie couldn't help but bring it up with Angus.

"Do you think it was a good idea for us to accept this invitation to Lady d'Orléac's party?"

"Why not? We had a good time, didn't we?"

"Yes, but... Lord Wanton advised you to avoid that family. I think that we should take his advice."

"Oh! Do you follow all of Timothy's advice?" asked Angus in a voice full of innuendos.

"No, I don't! Please, Angus, be serious for a moment."

"No, you're the one who should stop being serious for a moment, nightingale."

Elfie stopped, hesitated, and then went on, almost under her breath.

"It's just that I worry about Mr. Howard... What...? What does he want now?"

"Nothing, don't worry about it anymore. And let's not speak of it again," Angus added definitively. "Case closed."

To me, it doesn't seem like the case is closed from Howard's point of view, thought Elfie, who was still bothered by it all.

EPISODE 2

At Father Dupré's

Angus and Elfie took the Paris-Lyon train and went down to Yonne, about hundred miles southeast of Paris. They were expected at the home of the sculptor Dupré, who invited his friends every summer to stay at his widowed father's spacious home. Located on the village square in Saint-Julien-du-Sault, just across from the church, the house was large enough to accommodate his friends.

Fanny, Dupré's mistress and model, was already there. Fanny's sister Amandine had come with the sculptor Caron, who was a friend of Dupré's. The poet Vuillon and his companion Marie-Thérèse, a painter, who were both in their fifties, were also spending the summer at Father Dupré's house. Only Mr. Lenoir-Coty and Violette Roi were missing, and they would stop by for only a few days.

Mr. Dupré loved to host and would have happily invited all his son's friends for three or four months during the warm season. But his means wouldn't allow for that. So his son, the sculptor, had established a system where every morning, each guest would leave his contribution in a common jar in the kitchen, which was made available to the cook who provided the household with simple yet hearty meals. Their gracious host's wine flowed freely at these meals— his precious juice and the milk from his slopes, as he liked to call it.

The heat, that spring of 1866, was sweltering. So every afternoon, around four o'clock, a big cart with benches was hitched up and everyone took off in a joyous quest for some cool air beneath the poplars that lined banks of the Yonne River. They brought a picnic for later in the afternoon, including bottles of wine and canteens of water that they kept cool by submerging in the flowing river water. Marie-Thérèse took her sketchbook with her. For the first few days, Doreen, Elfie's lady's maid, sat up on the driver's bench next to the sculptor Dupré, who drove the old horse with a steady hand. He had spent his childhood leading this same cart for his father when he helped him work the fields. After that, Doreen preferred to walk along the banks of the Yonne, for one of the traveling journeymen, who were staying at the *Bons Enfants* Inn on the village square, always managed to slip away from his work at that time in order to accompany her.

The women wore wide-brimmed straw hats they had purchased at the open air market on the Saint-Julien-du-Sault village square. The men, in shirtsleeves, with vests unbuttoned, conversed in a casual and friendly manner. Elfie hit it off with Marie-Thérèse, whose paintings she admired. So she invariably sat next to her to chat with her.

On the very first day, Fanny and Amandine, who were used to undressing to pose for the artists, took off their dresses and waded deep into the cold water of the Yonne wearing only their chemises and drawers. They were soon joined by Angus, who jumped into the water completely naked. Fanny and Amandine's alert eyes took in every detail of his powerful virility before he dove in. Dupré, Caron, and Vuillon went for a swim too, but kept on their undergarments— not all men were totally devoid of modesty like Angus King.

Elfie stayed quietly by Marie-Thérèse, who took up her sketchbook and drew the bathers. The two models, both in their twenties, were very graceful, voluptuous young women of ample proportions. Violette, who was not much older, kept at a distance. Elfie didn't even remove her ankle boots, despite Angus's repeated appeals.

The next day, despite her reservations, Elfie couldn't resist. The heat was truly unbearable and the obvious pleasure felt by the bathers in the Yonne tempted her mightily. She took off her dress, embarrassed by her body that, compared to the two magnificent models, seemed skinny in spite of its evident curves. But she was sixteen and had not finished blossoming. In her chemise and drawers, she made her way down the grassy riverbank, in the shade of the tall poplars, taking careful steps for fear of some nasty little hidden critter. She folded her arms across her chemise to hide her chest. Fanny and Amandine were already in the water, splashing Angus to tease him. They knew, like everyone else, Angus's nature. But King's plan was working like a charm. Thanks to Elfie, he had managed to put people off his trail, even among his closest friends, and the two flirty sisters would have readily slipped off with him beneath the poplar trees.

Angus came toward the riverbank.

"What are you waiting for to come swimming, nightingale?"

"I'll get my feet wet, Angus. It's very cool here in the shade. I'm fine here."

In one leap, King straightened up his burly, dripping body out of the water, grabbed her by the waist, and pulled her into the river. She cried out in surprise, alarmed at seeing his impressive anatomy up close and scared of drowning. Angus pulled her into the water where she could no longer stand. Elfie clung to him as if he were a life preserver.

"Take me back, Angus! I'm scared!" she cried, hugging Angus's neck with her slender arms. "I'm scared!"

"Scared of what?" he laughed. "You're the one scaring me; you're going to strangle me!"

"We're going to drown!"

"No, we won't. I can still stand and I know how to swim."

Everyone in the water as well as on the riverbank was laughing at the prank Angus was playing on Elfie.

"Angus, I've never bathed in more water than my full bathtub. I can't see anything; where are my feet?"

"At the end of your legs, princess!" shouted Fanny, prompting general hilarity.

Princess was the nickname that the two sisters had affectionately given Miss Montesquiou, who was the only one staying at Father Dupré's to have her own lady's maid.

"What if the fish come and eat my feet?"

"Little fish don't eat big ones!" exclaimed Angus.

"Except in the Yonne River, Elfie," cried Amandine. "There are some very old fish that are bigger than you!"

"Is that true? Ah! Angus! I felt something! What was it?"

"Undoubtedly the same thing that Mr. King had you feel last night, princess!" called Fanny.

"A really big fish!" added Amandine.

Elfie calmed down, at least enough to avoid drawing everyone's attention, and loosened her grip on Angus's neck. He took her two hands and held her above the water, facing him.

"I'm floating!" she realized with surprise.

Angus, still holding her at arm's length, stepped further back.

"How do you like being in the water?" he asked.

"I like it. This heat is so unbearable. But I don't like this feeling... of not being in control, not knowing what is happening under my feet. What if it's full of strange animals, unknown and dangerous aquatic creatures?"

He smiled and continued to walk Elfie around in the water, slowly. The flow of the current drew their eyes downstream, so the riverbank on the other side seemed to be traveling upstream. The tender green leaves in the tall poplars trembled in the slight breeze, sparrows darted industriously around in the bushes to find food for their young, and larks grazed the water to take a drink or gulp down a few unlucky or distracted insects. Elfie relaxed.

"Perhaps some mermaids swam up from the sea, by way of the Seine River, to relax here in the Yonne?"

"I hope not! They would mistake you for one of their own and carry away my little alibi."

Coming out of the water, contrary to what Elfie expected, was much less enjoyable than going in. Her soaking chemise and drawers stuck to her body, accentuating her curves even more than if she had been naked. None of the men present held back from studying every last detail of her soft contours. *If I had agreed to the lessons that Lord Wanton offered me*, thought Elfie, *might I be better prepared to brave these looks?* Luckily, Doreen hurried over with a bath sheet and the men cursed this overzealous lady's maid.

"You must consider giving your lady's maid the day off tomorrow, mademoiselle!" sang out Mr. Lenoir-Coty, and was immediately smacked on the arm by Violette Roi, who didn't appreciate that her lover was ogling another woman right in front of her.

Violette and the two sisters, Fanny and Amandine, got along well together. The trio often went off to the only dry goods store in the village. Elfie sometimes accompanied them, but spending an hour debating the merits of a ribbon or a hat bored her exceedingly.

Elfie preferred Marie-Thérèse's company. The silent painter, very tall and thin, wore no hoop skirt and covered her lightweight dress with a long painter's apron. Interestingly, she had started out as a model thirty years earlier. She was quiet and secretive, but painted with incredible strength. She had set up her studio in a part of Mr. Dupré's stable that opened up toward the back yard and no longer stabled any horses except the old cart horse that would soon be retired. It was cool in the stables and the view was very pleasant. The yard was a simple square of bright green grass, enclosed on three sides by a wall of mossy gray stones as tall as a man and bordered with plump hydrangeas and fluttering cosmos.

Marie-Thérèse sometimes painted the garden, sometimes the bathers that she had sketched on the banks of the Yonne. She spoke little, but had heard Elfie converse with the men sitting around the table after eating and judged her presence acceptable. So Elfie would settle down to read in this stable-studio after the noon meal. Meanwhile everyone inside the house was taking a nap, sculpting, writing, posing, or resting.

One day, Elfie brought some blank paper and an ink pot to note down some of the conversations she had heard earlier that day. She got as comfortable as she could on a straw bale and put her ink pot on a crate that she had placed in front of her. This little setup that she had come up with and put into practice completely on her own filled her with happiness. It was silly, but never before in her life had she been allowed to arrange her own living space. It seemed to her that she had accomplished something, that she was taking charge of herself and leading her life as she pleased.

"I hope this won't bother you, Marie-Thérèse? Angus is taking a nap. He snores so loudly that I can't concentrate."

"No, it doesn't bother me at all. It's a good idea."

Three days later, Marie-Thérèse surprised her by having a little table brought in to serve as a desk. While one painted, the other read or wrote. From time to time, they exchanged a few words.

Habits were thus formed while staying at Father Dupré's. Elfie and Angus shared a large bedroom with whitewashed walls, furnished with one bed, one desk, a dresser, and a wardrobe. The adjoining water closet had only the bare minimum, but Elfie made do. The intimacy between the writer and his alibi grew. Angus never knocked before entering the room when Elfie was there, and he often walked around completely unclothed while she was writing at the desk. She called him to task for his numerous times, but then gave up and simply closed her eyes.

Angus King loved men, eating, drinking, writing, walking around naked in his room, and dressing extravagantly to draw everyone's attention. And although he was rather full of himself and loved having the last word, he never mocked or belittled Elfie's thoughts. Such was the man with whom Miss Montesquiou lived, and it suited her. Happy with the life of freedom she was leading, she was content with her lot.

EPISODE 3

The Jeweler

Father Dupré had gotten into the habit of letting travelers stay at his house. It helped him makes ends meet and gave him company at mealtimes. He was a *nice* man, as Elfie would say. No other word better described him, even

Angus had to admit. Dupré loved to have guests at his table, for as much as he loved the wine he had *suckled* since his early childhood, he loved to share it even more. He sat at the head of the table, a large white cotton napkin spread out over his chest, tucked under his beard and covering his enormous paunch. He uncorked a large number of bottles at every meal and invited his guests to serve themselves as much as they wanted.

Angus was happy to do just that, but as for Elfie, she had trouble finishing even one glassful.

"Water," Father Dupré had clearly explained, "is useless. It's only good for snails and fish!"

How does one dare to ask for water after that?

Three days after Elfie and Angus arrived, a young man named Pierre Pastel showed up at Father Dupré's house on his way to Paris.

Pierre had been apprenticed to his father, a jeweler in the town of Orange, for eleven years, ever since he was ten years old. Pastel's clients came to him for everything from having a baptismal spoon made or engraved, as a silversmith might do, to repairing a clock, as a clock maker might do. In the provinces, you had to know how to do a bit of everything: designing, mounting, setting, and polishing the piece, as well as engraving it. For an apprentice, there was nothing better. Pierre was familiar with the entire process and knew every step of making a piece of jewelry.

Pierre was ambitious and had decided to try his luck in Paris. He had left on foot for the capital, only sparingly dipping into the little purse his father had given him. A handsome young man, thin, with long, well-groomed hands and large brown eyes, he smiled at the drop of a hat. Women as well as men found him to be physically attractive. Pierre knew his own worth. The only obstacle he could see on his path forward was his timidity.

Pierre asked Father Dupré if he could stay in his stable. The weather was lovely and warm, and the river was not far. A hearty soup and a patch of straw would do just fine for a night, and would cost him very little money.

Elfie went to the stables to read in peace. Marie-Thérèse wasn't there, but her easel and box of paints were in their usual spot.

In a corner of the stable, Pierre had made a bed for himself with his blanket thrown over the straw, with his travel pack and vest carefully folded up next to it. Perched on a nearby straw bale was a closed wooden box containing his little collection of tools and a leather satchel from which a piece of paper had escaped. Elfie picked it up, intending to protect it from potentially being snatched up by a mouse or blown away by a gust of wind.

It was a design for a set of jewelry, drawn in ink and painted with perfect execution and beautiful attention to detail. Elfie had never seen anything like it. The strokes were sure-handed and the concept was totally different from previously-known designs. Although done in ink, in black and white, one could easily imagine what this jewelry might look like in gold and precious gemstones: the ears of wheat that formed the necklace were so meticulously drawn that one could almost see them rippling in the wind. Elfie lifted up the flap on the leather satchel to put the paper back inside, but when she saw that it contained many other designs, she couldn't resist taking a few out to look at them. After all, there was nothing wrong with admiring such beautiful work…

"I would have shown them to you if you had asked!" declared Pierre Pastel, who had come into the stable behind her.

Elfie jumped and spun around. It was the first time she had seen the young man. He was of medium height, without being short, slender, had a keen face with delicate features, a gentle expression in his eyes and a smile upon his thin, pink lips.

"Please excuse me, sir. I… I had no intention of… of poking through your things," she stammered uneasily. "I saw that a design had fallen out, and I picked it up to put it back safely and…"

"You saw the others!"

"Yes, I did."

"What did you think of them?"

"They are incredible! What talent."

"Thank you, mademoiselle. Let me introduce myself. I am Pierre Pastel."

"Oh, yes. I am Elfie Montesquiou."

"Delighted to meet you, mademoiselle."

"Are you staying here?"

"Yes, but only for one night. I am on my way to Paris. I am a jeweler and I am expected at Lemonnier's."

"Really? Why?"

"To make jewelry! That's my job."

"You make the jewelry that you invent and design, like these?"

"I have already done so, but on a small scale and not yet under my own name. But that's what I'll do as soon as I have my own studio. In the meantime, I sell my designs to other jewelers."

"They need a jeweler here in Saint-Julien-du-Sault. I broke my bracelet yesterday and couldn't find anyone to repair it."

"I can fix it for you, if that would be of help to you, mademoiselle. And I'll even do it for free."

"You need a workshop and tools, I presume?"

Pierre opened his wooden tool box.

"Look, I have enough tools in here for a small repair."

"That's so ni… you are very helpful, sir, but I dare not bother you with it."

"I've been walking all alone for days. I've decided to take a day of rest, but I'm a bit bored, I must say."

"Well then, in that case, I'll go up and get my bracelet and bring it to you!"

"Thank you, mademoiselle. I'll wait for you here. And feel free to call me Pierre. You can call me sir when I've been appointed as jeweler to Empress Eugenie!"

"When that happens, I won't call you anything anymore."

"Why not?"

"You'll be too expensive for me!"

They were both laughing as she left.

When Elfie entered their room, Angus was writing.

"I'm only passing through," she said, taking her bracelet out of her jewelry box.

"Isn't that bracelet broken?"

"Yes, but Pierre is going to fix it for me."

"Who is Pierre?"

"The young man who's staying in the stables."

"Do you know him?"

"Yes, I do. He's a jeweler and he offered to fix it for me," she declared, proud of her discovery.

Angus began to laugh.

"You're going to give your gold bracelet with emeralds that, although small, are still quite valuable, to a vagabond in the stables? And when is he going to give it back to you?"

"Tomorrow morning, I think. It depends on how long it takes him to repair it."

"You are so naive, Elfie! Tomorrow morning, he will be gone, along with your jewelry!"

Standing in the doorway, bracelet in hand, she hesitated. Such an attractive, friendly young man couldn't be a swindler.

"No, he won't, Angus! You see the bad in everything. He's

a very upstanding young man, I assure you."

"And you've known him for how long?"

"… Five minutes," she admitted.

"Don't follow through with this."

"…I most certainly will! I'm going to give him my bracelet!"

"Alright, since you are so gullible, I'm going with you, and if I don't like the look of him, you're not giving your bracelet to him."

"That's fine. But I'm sure you're going to like Pierre Pastel, Angus."

Down in the stable, Pierre had carefully set out a few tools on a wooden plank while he waited for Elfie to return. As soon as he saw her, he stood up politely.

"Mr. Pastel," said Elfie, "May I introduce Angus King, my travel companion."

The young man's eyes bulged like marbles.

"Mr. King, the writer?"

"The very same, young man," said Angus as he held out his hand, pleasantly intrigued.

"It's an honor for me to shake your hand, Mr. King," said Pierre with feeling.

"Would you like to show your designs to Angus, Mr. Pastel?" asked Elfie.

"Yes, of course I would, mademoiselle."

While the young man opened his satchel, Elfie glanced at

Angus, who only had eyes for Pierre. In spite of her limited experience, she could tell that something had clicked between the two men.

EPISODE 4

The Unlikely Couple

Without a word, Angus looked at the designs that Pierre handed him one by one while giving a few explanations about the technical aspects of his work. The cool air of the stables suddenly seemed more like a breath of hot wind blowing in from the desert. Elfie didn't know whether she should leave or stay. One thing was certain, she had become a third wheel. But she thought of Marie-Thérèse, who might arrive at any moment at the stable to paint, and wasn't she, Elfie, the alibi?

"Aren't Mr. Pastel's designs wonderful, Angus?" she asked cheerfully.

The two men looked up at her, surprised by her presence.

"Yes, they certainly are," replied Angus. "You will go far, young man. Elfie, what are you waiting for? Don't you have a bracelet that needs to be fixed?"

Elfie smiled. It was amazing how Angus's suspicions had melted away so quickly!

"Of course. Here, Mr. Pastel. Do you think you can do something with it?"

"May I?"

He sat down at his improvised workbench and examined the bracelet.

"One hour of work at the very most, mademoiselle," he quoted professionally.

Angus pulled up two straw bales so that he and Elfie could sit and watch Pierre as he set to work.

"Elfie told me that you are leaving tomorrow?" Angus asked the young man.

"Alas, yes, Mr. King. I must arrive at Mr. Lemonnier's in ten days, and I think it will take me five days to walk there. And I should find a place to stay in Paris before I start work, while I still have the time."

Pierre leaned over his work once again. Angus discreetly elbowed Elfie. She looked up at him; he was making breaststroke motions in the air and looking pointedly at Pierre, silently signaling her to invite him to join them for swimming later that afternoon. Elfie stared at him with wide eyes, clearly indicating the message, *Do it out yourself!* when Marie-Thérèse came in.

"Hello! Is this now the latest salon for visiting?"

Angus rose to his feet.

"Why, yes, it is. Believe it or not, ma'am, this young man

is a talented jeweler. He's repairing Elfie's bracelet."

Marie-Thérèse removed the sheet that was covering her easel and began preparing her palette.

"I know. Pierre and I met this morning. His designs are admirable."

"Thank you, ma'am," said Pierre.

"Elfie wanted to invite her talented jeweler to join us for swimming later, as a way of thanking him," Angus blurted out. "Would that be alright with you, Marie-Thérèse?"

"What a good idea, Elfie. Pierre, my charming stable companion, you are welcome to join our little party."

"I accept with pleasure. Thank you, ma'am."

Angus looked at Elfie, beaming with the superior air of a man who had won this round. She narrowed her eyes and shot him a waspish look, taking her revenge by saying, "Very well, I'll leave you two now. See you later, Marie-Thérèse."

As she left the stable, she knew that Angus would not stay there alone with Pierre and would be forced to leave as well, which he did.

"Yes, let's go, Elfie."

Pierre thought he would leave the next day, but he hadn't counted on meeting Angus King, and ended up spending more than a week in the stable, happier than he ever had been before.

Elfie and Angus went back to their room to get ready to go swimming.

"May I know why you shot me such a nasty look?"

"I don't like it when you use me, Angus."

"To invite Pierre?"

"So, in the blink of an eye, he went from *that vagabond* to Pierre?"

"Yet another thing I didn't foresee about our deal, nightingale."

"What's that?"

"That we might be in competition with each other! Did you want to keep Pierre all to yourself?"

"But…! Of course not! What an idea!"

"Well then, what's the problem? You're my alibi, right?"

"Yes, I am," Elfie agreed. "You're right. I'm only here to cover for you."

"Then we are in agreement!" Angus exclaimed happily.

But Elfie remained preoccupied.

"Come on, alibi, don't make that face. We're going to have a wonderful time here!"

"Hmm. And we'll go back to Paris after our stay here?"

"No, we're going to Italy, as planned. Why?"

"I thought that maybe… no, nothing."

"Whatever happens, Pierre is only passing by on our path. He's going north and we're going south. I'm going to offer to buy him a train ticket to Paris so that he can extend his stay here."

"He seems to be a very proud person. He won't accept."

"You're right. But I'll find a way to convince him to stay longer."

"But… what about Lord Wanton?"

Angus smiled.

"There is not only one way of living, nightingale. Besides, Timothy has but to cross the Channel, if he wants to keep an eye on me! My plan is to take advantage of the good things that life has to offer; I am only too familiar with nasty surprises that might hit at any moment, without warning. And…" he added with amusement, "you're in quite the position to understand the limits of Lord Wanton's faithfulness, you little hypocrite."

"Angus! I… I…"

"Come on, enjoy it like I do, nightingale! Right across the village square, staying at the *Bons Enfants* Inn, there are twenty young, handsome, single traveling journeymen who, at the snap of your fingers would be happy to wrap themselves around your little finger… or the rest of you!"

"Angus! I… I…"

"You're repeating yourself! Come on, let's go down to the dining room and see if they others are ready to leave!"

Arm in arm, they entered the dining room, Elfie's cheeks still blushing from Angus's innuendos. Vuillon, the poet, raised his wine glass and recited:

"Welcome, you unlikely couple
Finally awake from your nap!
The singer's body is supple,
Angus, you're a lucky old chap.
Elfie enjoys calligraphy,
Angus prefers pornography!
Blame it on his sweet companion
If Angus shows agitation
How you, eccentric Angus,
Could entice this prim little miss
From her prayers to your kisses
And into the arms of Bacchus?
Impervious to the rumor,
The pretty couple, with humor,
Will still be hungry for bread
After their tumble in bed!
Angus with his stout massive frame,
Consorts with the princess, behold!
And thanks to her love all aflame,
Like the goddess of love she is bold."

As bright red as a poppy, Elfie hid her face in Angus's shirt.

"Wine always inspires the best poetry!" cried Angus. "Father Dupré, please pour me a glass, before we head out to the river."

They all went out to the village square to wait for the cart and then piled in, still laughing giddily over Vuillon's poem. Pierre Pastel also appeared timidly on the terrace, not daring to impose. Angus glanced at Elfie, who called out to him.

"Mr. Pastel, we'll take you with us! Climb on up!" she said, patting the place on the bench next to her.

Pierre climbed up and thanked her as he sat down.

"Oh, better watch out, King!" exclaimed the sculptor Caron. "Women always end up preferring the handsome ones."

"I'm not worried!" said Angus, putting his arm around Elfie's shoulders. "Sing us a song, please, nightingale," he asked to change the conversation.

In keeping with the prevailing mood of frivolity, Elfie began:

Madame Arthur is quite the lady
They chatter and chatter about her all over Paris
She may be mature and slightly shady
But each man is her lover-to-be
They line up in rows to implore her
To deck her in jewels they're keen.
And why do they madly adore her?
It's her— well, you know what I mean!

Madame Arthur is quite the lady
They chatter and chatter about her all over Paris

*She may be mature and slightly shady
But each man is her lover-to-be
Madame Arthur is quite the lady.
They talk about her all over Paris!*

*Of average height, average complexion
Her eyes have a sparkle that's sometimes a tiresome tease
Though her voice is sweet, her inflection
Would not charm the birds off the trees.
Her figure's a bit on the slack side
Of beauty she's hardly the queen
But when you get a view of her backside
She shows— well, you know what I mean!*

*Madame Arthur is quite the lady
They chatter and chatter about her all over Paris
She may be mature and slightly shady
But each man is her lover-to-be
Madame Arthur is quite the lady.
They talk about her all over Paris!*

*Her lovers all stay faithful to her
It's her whim and her whim alone that can send them away
She maintains that old love can't renew her
She needs a new lover each day.
And each lover, as he is rejected,
Of the new man with envy is green
Other women just leave him dejected
They don't have— well, you know what I mean!*

*You should have seen her dancing;
She always gave it her all
Swaying to and fro and prancing,
She was the queen of the ball
Her feet kicked as high as her face*

More partners have never been seen
Everyone cheered, my, what grace!
And my, what— well, you know what I mean!

And how did this lady get by?
With such an elegant household
Through farce and tragedies too
She remained center-stage, I am told
As for paying her rent when due
She remained in a state quite serene
For her landlord, she knew very well
Admired her— well, you know what I mean!

Ladies, if you, like her, are longing
To have man after man after man after man on a string:
They will never come around you thronging
Unless you have one certain thing.
It's neither your grace nor your bearing.
It isn't your skin's healthy sheen
Your clothes, or the perfume you're wearing.
It's your— well, you know what I mean!"

Angus smiled, speechless in amazement. Fanny, Amandine, and Violette joined in on the refrains. They arrived on the banks of the Yonne and the men took the women by the waists to help them down from the cart.

"Where did that song come from, you sly and secretive little imp?" asked Angus, leading Elfie away from the others beneath the poplar trees.

"It's one of the first street songs I ever learned by heart, after hearing our own cook sing it around the kitchen, back at my father's house in Clamart. I must have been seven or eight years old. It was one of the first songs I sang around the house, very proud of myself, to my family, without understanding what it meant. For that little performance,

I spent two long days locked up in my room. After which my father released me, with a sententious 'I hope you have learned your lesson!' I said yes, of course, because I knew that was what I was supposed to say. But I had no idea why I wasn't supposed to sing that song."

Angus smiled.

"And now you have some idea why, nightingale?"

"Vaguely, Angus."

EPISODE 5

Leading Separate Lives

They swam and had a great time. Fanny and Amandine gently pestered Pierre to join in, but were unsuccessful, and he instinctively sought refuge with Elfie, who sat at a slight distance from the others.

"So you are going to be hired by a jeweler in Paris?"

"Yes, at Lemonnier's. Are you familiar with them?"

"Yes, I've heard the name," replied Elfie noncommittally, remembering how expensive the jewelry was at Lemonnier's— well beyond her means. "It's highly reputable."

"You see, mademoiselle, in the great studios like Mr. Lemonnier's, the workers are specialized in one of the several, quite distinct steps in the fabrication of a piece of jewelry: the design, the mounting, the setting, the polishing, and the engraving. But I know how to do it all. And in addition, I plan on selling my designs to any jeweler who wants to buy them. By designing in the evenings after work, I'll earn more and will quickly build up a reputation, and then I'll open my own studio."

Pierre Pastel impressed Elfie. He was totally paralyzed when women teased him, but so sure of himself when he talked about his work.

"Would you have time, outside of all that work, to create pieces for individual clients?"

"I would welcome the opportunity, but for now I have absolutely no client base."

"Of course you do— what about me? I admit that I don't have many contacts. But Mr. King frequents the most exclusive salons, and when I get compliments on my jewelry, I'll be sure to tell people who made it. Perhaps that could be your first step on the ladder to success? It would be an honor for me to wear your creations. Your designs are amazing."

"I could take on individual orders in addition to my work, of course. But I don't have the cash flow to finance even the smallest of orders."

"I'll pay you in advance and you can procure whatever you see fit."

"Mademoiselle, this is beyond my wildest hopes!"

"There is only one problem, which is that you won't be able to make your beautifully designed sets for me."

"I'll design some pieces that will fit your budget."

Elfie smiled and held out her hand.

"In that case, you have your first client, Mr. Pastel!"

Pierre shook her hand happily.

"Thank you, mademoiselle."

"I'll give you the money for my first order before you leave. Mr. King and I should be returning to Paris at the end of August, I think."

Emile de Chabanais, the director of the *Free Thought?* newspaper, had a subscription to Thomas Ink's *Monthly Thoughts*. That way, Chabanais kept abreast of the current trends in British and American thought. Of course he had read the articles by Life Emotions and had sent a letter to Saint-Julien-du-Sault addressed directly to Elfie.

Dear Miss Montesquiou,

I recently read three articles in Monthly Thoughts *signed Life Emotions, with whom you are familiar, I presume?*
I am extremely vexed that a fellow countryman did not first seek to publish his articles in my newspaper Free Thought?*, which, as I mentioned to you, is looking for young journalists. I am convinced that this author is indeed French, for one or two turns of phrase in his article bore the unmistakable mark of Angus King's quill.*
If, by chance, mademoiselle, you happen to meet this Life Emotions, feel free to point him in my direction. Who knows if I would be able to forgive him for selling himself to the English before coming to find me, but perhaps I could publish him if his prose in French is promising?

Respectfully yours,
Emile de Chabanais

P.S. Would you please be so kind as to remind King that I am still waiting for his next article in the series that he promised me?

"Angus! Angus!" cried Elfie, barging into their room.

"What is it?" he asked in alarm.

"Read this! Read, while I get to work! Can you believe it? If Mr. de Chabanais were to publish my work...?"

Elfie left her sentence hanging and sat down at the desk. She opened her ink pot, took out a sheet of paper, and, ignoring Angus who was reading her letter, started talking to herself.

"What if I could manage to earn enough money, like you, Angus! I would be free!"

King, behind her, lowered his arm with the letter still in hand and watched her dip her quill into the ink pot, surprised by what she had said. Elfie looked over at him, her face awash with happiness.

"How much can I hope to get paid in France? Will you help me negotiate the rate, Angus?"

"Don't get ahead of yourself!" he retorted, suddenly in a bad mood. "Wait and see if Emile accepts your article. Besides, I have my own work to do, so figure it out on your own!"

Elfie went back to her writing. She was used to no longer paying much attention to King's mood swings.

Angus King had always traveled alone and it had always suited him just fine. But it wasn't until Elfie had implied that someday she might make her own way in the world, separate from him, that he realized how much he had started to like not being alone anymore. Outside of Lord Wanton, he had never gotten attached to any man. He sometimes teased Timothy for not wanting to step foot in a boat, but deep down, their arrangement pleased him. Who knows how long their relationship would have lasted if they had lived together?

With Elfie, it was different. Their relationship was nothing but a mutual agreement. And she didn't hinder his precious freedom, for he was the one who paid her wages. He knew that she put up with his bad moods, followed him wherever he went even if it wasn't where she wanted to go, and kept her own worries to herself so as not to bother him, only because she didn't have any other choice for the time being. She never complained and cheerfully made the best of everything with the discipline of a young lady who was raised to stoically endure the whims of men.

Up until now, Angus had taken advantage of his alibi, thinking that he was good to her, and with the clear conscience of a man who pays fairly for a job well done. They discussed things as equals, which very few women were lucky enough to experience, and he sincerely liked her. He looked at his little nightingale's face as she sat at the desk and concentrated on her writing, so happy at the thought of being able to take flight with her own wings. He finally understood that there was an imbalance in their relationship that was not to Elfie's advantage. If not, she wouldn't be so thrilled at the thought of leaving him.

When Angus had found Timothy in Elfie's room several weeks earlier, he had flown into a rage. A little thorn had stuck him in the foot and he had yanked it out without a second thought. Being faithful was not in any way expected in his relationship with Timothy, for either of them, and that suited them both just fine. But now, in this room in Saint-Julien-du-Sault, the thorn rankled again and he knew why he had gotten angry at Elfie and Timothy. He didn't care if Lord Wanton was dallying with his nightingale. What had upset him was the realization that Elfie might someday get attached to another man. Angus had gotten used to his nightingale's company and could no longer imagine traveling without her. Which is what would happen if Elfie flew off on her own.

But their deal clearly stipulated that each of them could lead their own lives as they please, and Angus had better get used to the idea. Would he be able to allow Elfie the freedom to make her own choices in the future? He promised himself to take some time to think about this, but their stay in Yonne kept him busy with other things.

That evening, Angus went to find Pierre in the stable. By the light of an oil lamp, he was intent on his drawing. The soft, fine tip of his paintbrush slid silently over the blank white page, leaving jewels of black ink in its wake, the inverse of a brilliant white trail of a falling star against the black night sky.

"Am I bothering you, Pierre?" asked Angus.

"I was hoping you'd come, Mr. King," replied Pierre.

Angus came closer and blew out the oil lamp. Pierre stood up. They waited for a few seconds, long enough for their eyes to adjust to the faint light of the quarter moon.

King leaned slightly toward Pierre and kissed him on the lips.

"One night won't be enough, Pierre," he said, sitting down on the blanket.

"It's all I have to give, Mr. King."

"Accept my offer for a train ticket to Paris. That will give you several more days here."

"No, I couldn't."

"You don't want to stay here with me for a few days?"

"Yes, I do, I want nothing more. But I don't want you to give me money."

"Can you see well enough to write a letter?"

"Yes, why?"

"Take out a sheet of paper, I'll dictate."

Pierre took out a blank page from his satchel, reopened his little ink pot, and dipped his quill in.

"I, the undersigned, Pierre Pastel, dated blablablah..." Angus began, "certify having received from Mr. Angus King the amount of two hundred francs and hereby agree to repay this amount with interest before the month of June 1869. Signed, etc..."

Pierre had written everything down as dictated. He hesitated and set down his quill pen.

"Go on, sign it!" said Angus. "With this IOU, you'll have a clear conscience and three years to pay me back. Although, I won't ever come back to hound you for something this trivial!"

Pierre dipped his quill into the black ink and held it above the paper for a moment.

"For pity's sake, sign it!" implored Angus.

The young man drew a swirly P as beautiful as a tropical bird and signed it.

By morning, Angus had placed Elfie's bracelet on her

nightstand, as good as new after Pierre's repairs.

EPISODE 6

The Traveling Journeymen

On Sunday, as they headed down toward their usual spot on the banks of the Yonne River, as they did every afternoon, they saw a group of young men who were already swimming a little further downstream. They were traveling journeymen who would have no doubt loved it if a few young women from the village had joined them, but they knew that this was but a pipe dream. The young men in the villages they passed through were leery of these strapping lads who had gained confidence by traveling all around France learning their trades and were therefore irresistibly attractive to the young ladies of the village. One wink, after a few beers, was enough to trigger a fist fight.

When her friends had stretched out on the grass, after finishing their food and drink, Elfie had to distance herself for a moment, and went into the bushes out of eyesight of the others. As she came back toward the riverbank to join her little group, she passed right by the path leading from the Yonne River up to the open-air dancing hall. Looking out from behind the trees that hid her, she could see the young journeymen shouting as they emerged from the water— all their clothing had disappeared except their caps and hats. They had no choice but to go back into town naked, completely bare except their heads— so at least their dignity would remained intact!

"I see we have the same tastes!" whispered King into Elfie's ear.

Elfie started, caught in the act of voyeurism.

"Oh, no, I... I just had to..."

Angus burst out laughing at his young friend's flustered face. Immediately, the young men caught sight of them. They were laughing and jostling each other like little kids, quickly covering their genitals with cupped hands and looking around for a place to hide. Then, in a show of bravado, they changed their minds. They puffed out their muscular chests, held their young chins high, and passed right in front of the young woman and the man. They were naked, but proud, each one tipping his cap or hat politely to Elfie, who kept her head and eyes lowered chastely while Angus continued to laugh.

"You're not very sneaky!" she burst out once the men were out of sight. "You gave us away!"

She grabbed her skirts, hiking them up to her knees and took off running back to the others, picking up her feet high amid the tangled weeds. Angus followed, as delighted as Elfie was after that fortunate encounter!

A week later, Elfie and Angus walked with Pierre to the Saint-Julien-du-Sault train station. On their way back, Angus didn't take the path toward the house on the square. He wanted to take the long way.

Elfie, walking behind him, did not disturb his thoughtful silence. With great nervous steps, Angus trampled the grass growing up in the path. He picked up a small branch and whacked the nettles growing along the edge of the path, paying no attention to his alibi who followed along as best she could. Elfie racked her brain for a way to comfort him, and although she was getting tired from running behind Angus in the hot sun, she began to sing *À la claire Fontaine*:

"As I went a-walking
Near the fountain's rim
The water was inviting
So I went for a swim
I've loved you for so long, I'll never forget you
My friend has gone away
Unwanted was this end
But gold and precious gems
Wouldn't let him stay
I've loved you for so long, I'll never forget you
I wish that every gem
Stayed buried in the hill
And that my dear sweet friend
Was here to love me still
I've loved you for so long, I'll never forget you."

Picking up her pace so as not to lose sight of Angus, Elfie was slightly out of breath as she continued to sing softly. Suddenly turning around to face her, Angus shouted:

"Can't you leave me alone to my own thoughts for one

minute?"

Surprised by his aggressive tone of voice, Elfie looked up at Angus who started off walking again. Hurrying to keep up with him once again, she hit her shin on a stump. She let out a cry and leaned over to rub her painful leg.

"Can't you be more careful?" scolded Angus angrily.

Elfie knew that he was incapable of comforting others and that, being unaware of this, he lashed out instead of empathizing. But this time, she had really hurt herself.

"Don't say anything if you can't say something to comfort me!" she cried, on the verge of tears.

The pain was so sharp that she almost choked on it.

"Let's go home!" he roared.

They both made an effort to hide their feelings when they first got back to the house. Elfie because she was really in pain and because she was mad at Angus; Angus because he had to hide the pain that Pierre Pastel's departure caused him.

Elfie went straight up to their room. She sat down on the bed and removed her shoes and stockings, uncovering the nastiest bruise she had ever seen. She rested her leg on the bed, which eased the pain a bit by reducing the blood flow.

"Oh, that doesn't look good!" exclaimed Angus as he came in. "I had no idea it was so bad. I'll go get Doreen, maybe she'll know how to treat it."

"Thank you, Angus."

"I'm sorry you hurt your leg, nightingale."

"I'm sorry Pierre has gone."

"The bruise on my heart will heal just like the bruise on your leg!" he quipped before turning to leave.

"You have every right to feel sad, Angus."

"My religion forbids it!"

"If only my religion could forbid feeling pain!" grimaced

Elfie.

After Doreen had rubbed some ointment onto her mistress's leg, the writer came and laid down next to his alibi.

"I hear the others getting ready to go for a swim, Angus. I don't want to move, but you can go with them. Don't feel like you have to stay here and keep me company."

"I don't feel like I have to do anything, Elfie," he said sadly. "You should know that by now."

Elfie said nothing. What she knew was that it only took a fraction of a second for him to go from feeling sad over Pierre's departure to lashing out belligerently, which stemmed from his inability to confide in others.

"He's handsome, isn't he?" asked Angus, not bothering to say the name Pierre.

"Very handsome, yes," confirmed Elfie, who sincerely thought he was. "You know, Angus, the first time I saw Pierre, he reminded me of Michelangelo's *David*, which I saw of print of at Lord Wanton's."

"Yes, you're right. I should have been handsome, too. I'm jealous of his beauty. I'm ugly."

"Angus, you are not ugly!"

"Elfie, you are not a credible witness!"

They began to laugh.

"You shouldn't feel bad about not being handsome, Angus."

"What condescension from a young lady who is so pretty that every one of her partners begged for several dances at the dancing hall the other night!"

"If you think about it, Angus, since you love to be surrounded by beauty, your position is preferable to that of Pierre or Lord Wanton. You have handsome men to look at, while they have you to look at!"

"Your evasive reply only confirms what I said, nightingale!" smiled Angus, taking Elfie in his arms tenderly.

Elfie relaxed in his embrace, not at all angry that Pierre had left.

The Countess Graciosa had invited them to spend the summer at her villa in Tuscany, not far from Florence. When Angus had informed Elfie of this invitation, she had jumped for joy— a trip to Italy! Many of the English ladies and gentlemen she had met at Lord Wanton's had been shocked to hear she had never taken a trip to Italy, which was indispensable to any cultural education. They raved to Elfie about Italian cathedrals, museums, great Renaissance painters, charming inns, the narrow, shady streets where laundry was hung out to dry for all to see, and the *pensioni* lodgings... and you should have heard how they delighted in the sounds of that beautiful language.

"You'll see, miss, how picturesque Italy is!" one lady had exclaimed in Lord Wanton's drawing room as the rain drummed against the windows. "We would never dare to hang our laundry outside in England!"

"And for good reason!" Elfie had murmured to Lord Wanton, causing him to smile.

The men whispered among themselves about their delicious memories of plump Italian women, while others more privately remembered the golden skin of certain young Italian men...

Angus King had not gone back to Italy for several years, so the trip had tempted him. On the other hand, he had explained to Elfie, you never knew what kind of guests to expect at Lady Graciosa's. And Angus absolutely refused to spend time with annoying people.

"This past winter, at Timothy's, Graciosa didn't seem up to her usual form. Sure, she's the most beautiful hen in the barnyard, but I have no taste for poultry, except on my dinner plate."

"You're being mean, Angus," Elfie had said. "The Countess has other qualities. Let's go, please! Please?" she had begged.

"Why not? Besides, I think you're the one she wants to see, so you can entertain her with your singing. I thought you didn't want to sing on command? If we go, you'll have to put your talents on display every evening."

"Nothing ventured, nothing gained! A dozen or so songs for a trip to Italy seems fair! Besides, who knows, perhaps the Countess has invited some guests who are intelligent and cultivated enough to live up to your grandeur, Mr. King?" Elfie had teased.

"Wanton was right, you're becoming as sharp-tongued as an old English duchess! Very well, let's go to Italy! Maybe we'll see César de Beaumont there? The last letter I received from him was sent from Rome."

At the end of June, Angus and Elfie took the train to Marseille by way of Lyon and from there boarded a steamboat headed to Naples. Angus wanted to approach Italy from the magnificent Gulf of Naples, and then make their way slowly up to Florence by train, making stops wherever it struck their fancy.

EPISODE 7

Naples

The sun was low on the horizon over the beautiful, dark sapphire-blue of the Mediterranean Sea. The steamboat *Neptune* had already rounded the islands of Ischia and Procida and was heading straight into the Bay of Naples. The sun at their backs, the passengers could admire this magnificent bay with the city of Naples, lit up by the setting sun, nestled along its shoreline. The white houses dotting the nearly black mountainside were ablaze in the slanting orange rays. It was even more beautiful than how Elfie had imagined it.

The steamboat for Naples was carrying mostly English passengers, who naturally kept to themselves, like a superior caste or like vinegar on the surface of a flask of oil, railed Angus— which, in Elfie's view, wasn't flattering for either the English or the other passengers! Eyes on the shoreline, she didn't see the multitude of little skiffs and rowboats that had come out from the wharf and were launching their attack on the *Neptune*. She looked down and saw this crush of Neapolitan sailors only after she heard these men on their little colorful dinghies shouting and yelling among themselves and hollering up to the English tourists.

The red-faced lords and the ladies in their frilly white dresses, protected from the sun by their parasols on their first trip to Italy, huddled together on the deck reserved for the first class passengers. They looked like a flock of pink and white sheep penned in by these swarthy Italians in shirtsleeves, wearing rough canvas pants faded by the sun and held up by rope belts.

The *facchini*, or porters from the hotels, called out to them from water-level, clinging onto the *Neptune* and scrambling aboard by finding handholds and footholds wherever they could, like pirates boarding an enemy ship. There were so many hotels in Naples that they were fighting over their clients even before they had a chance to disembark.

At the Rome Hotel, Angus booked a spacious room for himself and Elfie, plus a small attic room for Doreen, to whom he gave a few coins for the porters. The lady's maid had their bags taken up and paid the porters. But the *facchini*, obviously not satisfied with this payment, vociferated their opinion with loud voices and energetic gestures. Doreen mustered up all her British composure to explain to them in her own language that they would not get a cent more, but to no avail. So she abandoned the affability she normally used in her work and used a more universal language— cursing at the porters and threatening them with her hand raised above her head, which sent the men running.

"And don't come back!" she shouted after them, underscoring her authority with a decisive bob of her head.

After spending three days at the Rome Hotel in Naples, Angus began to notice that Elfie's features were drawn and her mood was deteriorating. It was because she heard Angus go out every night and had picked up on the looks he exchanged with young Italian men. She was having trouble sleeping. As soon as she closed her eyes, that night in Folkestone came flooding back and the thought of Angus being imprisoned again haunted her dreams.

During their visit to the Pompeii ruins, Elfie had to stop and rest on a stone. Angus expressed his concerns. Elfie confided to him that his evening outings made her fear the worst. But he assured her that here in Italy, no one would bother either one of them. She was reassured, but as they were leaving the site, she sat down again.

"Come on, nightingale, we still have an hour's walk ahead of us," Angus said impatiently. "And I'm hungry!"

Angus King wasn't very good at tolerating things that annoyed him, but being hungry was especially unbearable for him. If he didn't sit down to eat as soon as his stomach called for food, he became insufferably grumpy.

"I'm sorry, Angus, but I'm tired. Plus, I have a blister on my right heel. It really hurts."

"You should have told me, I would have rented a donkey to come here."

"No, I'm glad you didn't. I normally like to walk, and besides I don't like riding on those beasts. They scare me."

"There is no reason to be scared. You had no trouble riding Timothy's mare, did you?"

"That's true, but my confidence had been boosted."

"By Timothy or by the mare?"

"Angus!"

"Hold on, I see a donkey tied up over there. I'll go see if his rider is nearby. Don't move."

"No, Angus, it won't do any good! I won't ride on a donkey."

But he had already left in search of the donkey. Elfie placed her foot on the ground, causing another sharp pain from her blister. She tried to loosen up her ankle boot to give her foot some relief.

When she looked up, Angus stood before her holding the donkey's bridle.

"Come on, climb up!"

"Where's the rider?"

"I couldn't find him."

"But, that's stealing!" she whispered.

"Borrowing, nothing more. I'll slip some money under the saddle and this hearty burrow will find his own way back to his master."

Angus promptly scooped up Elfie and put her on the donkey.

"Angus, let me down!"

But he caught hold of her unlaced boot, took it off her foot, and put it into his pocket.

"There. This way, your foot won't hurt anymore and you won't be able to get off your magnificent steed either!" he said with a laugh.

Elfie pursed her lips as a matter of form, but didn't say anything, as she was only too happy to be relieved of her pain. The animal, not used to being ridden by someone other than his master, at first refused to budge, but then, recognizing that he was dealing with someone more stubborn than himself, ended up deciding to move forward.

"Angus, this isn't right!"
"Does your foot hurt?"
"No, but still!"
"Enjoy it, then!"
She smiled, her spirits lifted.
Angus looked at her and said, "You naughty girl, aren't you ashamed to be breaking the rules and laughing about it, to boot!"
"Stop this donkey, I'm getting down!"
He burst out laughing and she couldn't help but laugh along with him.

That evening, in the hotel lobby, a pink-faced English man with white sideburns— who always bragged about what he had toured that day and how his experiences were always more beautiful, more extraordinary, and more delicious than anything the others might have done— told Elfie and Angus about his outrage when his guide's donkey had been stolen while he was visiting the ruins of Pompeii. He had to walk for miles before finding an alternative means of transportation!

As tourists, their lives drifted by peacefully and poetically, enlivened by pleasant surprises and lighthearted diversions. Elfie loved everything in Italy: the museums, the churches, the colorful noises of the Neapolitan workers — such as the public writers who opened up the wooden panels of their tiny shops and set up their table and chair, ink pot and paper, directly on the sidewalks; and the ice water vendors who called out to anyone and everyone to buy their water before it was hot enough to make tea; and the meat sellers stabbing their meat onto skewers before lighting their fires just in time for the meat to be cooked to perfection at noon. She especially loved the *San Carlo* opera house and the music of Rossini.

One evening, Angus took Elfie out to eat in an *osteria*. The sun was setting, bathing the ocher walls of the building in a rosy glow. On the plaza, a singer holding a mandolin wasn't far from their table. Angus, after the copious meal he had just ingested, was casually leaning back in his chair as he finished off his bottle of wine. At first, Elfie had been shocked at his gargantuan appetite, but she had eventually gotten used to it. She herself didn't eat much and sometimes waited around for an hour as her companion finished up all the dishes he had ordered.

"Nothing can satisfy a man who's languished for two years on a prison diet, Elfie!" he had explained to her.

She could have retorted that she had spent nine years eating with the nuns at boarding school, but she refrained.

While Elfie waited for Angus, who was admiring the color of his wine as the slanting rays of the setting sun filtered through it, Elfie learned a tarantella from the street singer, who charmed her with the smooth chords of his mandolin, his resonant voice, and his black velvet eyes.

The young singer's skin was browned by the sun like a forgotten piece of bread left in the back of a wood-burning oven by a distracted baker, and his tousled hair was as black as the hardened lava of Mt. Vesuvius. In shirtsleeves, he played his mandolin to a cheerful, lively rhythm. His feet were bare, but you couldn't tell at first because they were so swollen and calloused from the years of weathering and had long since taken on the color of dark leather shoes.

Elfie was the exact opposite. Her complexion was fair, for she kept her small face suitably protected from the sun by her white parasol. Her silky chestnut hair was pulled back into a pretty bun at the nape of her neck with ringlet curls bobbing above her shoulders. She squinted in the gentle Italian sunlight tinged with a golden hue that was matched by the golden flecks in her own green eyes.

The singer led Elfie a little away from their outdoor table at the *osteria* and out onto the plaza for a spontaneous concert. Their deep, warm voices were in perfect unison as they sang a tarantella— *La Danza* by Rossini— to the great enjoyment of all who happened to stroll by that evening.

EPISODE 8

The Nun's Legs

A few days later, Elfie was walking decisively along the wharf on her way to mail a letter. She was gazing out at the port of Naples, when she tripped over a coil of rope on the dock. Thrown off balance, she dropped the letter, which fluttered away. As Elfie chased after it, she jumped onto a floating dock made out of old, rotting wooden planks. The letter landed gently upon the green water of the harbor just as one of the deck boards gave way under Elfie's weight. Her leg went through up to her calf, the rotting wood tearing her stocking and the skin beneath it. She would have sunk completely into the water if a teenager, who had dived in to retrieve the letter, hadn't caught her in his arms. Supported by him, Elfie carefully extricated her leg and foot. From both sides of the floating dock, fishermen rushed over to help.

Now the men who had helped her back up to the wharf were surrounding her, gesticulating and shouting:

"Make room! Make room! A young lady is injured! Make way for a young foreigner who got hurt!"

Their grandiloquence was accompanied by a great waving of their muscular, tanned arms. Elfie vaguely understood that they meant well, but she would have preferred more discretion. After a lively discussion, two of them made a seat out of their four arms so that Elfie could sit and be carried. She was horribly embarrassed, but without waiting for her permission, they scooped her up and the procession moved off.

Elfie caught sight of Angus seated on the terrace of a little cafe. She called out to him, trying to catch his attention by raising her arm while also still holding on to the two men who were carrying her. But she was drowned out by this human tidal wave. And the hubbub of the crowd around her was so loud that even after Angus turned to look at this exuberant crowd, he didn't see her or hear her.

Finally Angus saw her. He stared at her for a second before he understood what was happening and jumped up in a great bound, roaring like an enraged lion whose prey is being stolen.

"That's my wife! Let her go! Let her go or I'll kick your asses!" he bellowed, striding over and brandishing his lion-handled cane over his head.

The crowd immediately shut up and the two men who were carrying Elfie set her gently on the ground.

"Everything's alright, Angus! *Gracie, gracie,*" thanked Elfie, turning toward the men who were shuffling away, disappointed at not being able to complete their mission.

Elfie grabbed onto Angus's arm to stand on her good foot and take the weight off her injured leg. Immediately, Angus leaned over, lifted up her skirt in the middle of the street, and saw her torn stocking reddened with blood.

"What happened?" he said with alarm.

She burst out laughing.

"Nothing! I was just trying to mail my letter! This letter," she added, showing him the scrap of crumpled, soggy paper in her hand. You couldn't make out any of the writing, for the ink had smeared into a blurry, black streak. "We're having fun here in Italy, don't you think, Angus?"

That very night, after Elfie implored him to not fuss over her, Angus went out with a few Englishmen who were passing through town.

He came back rather late and found Elfie asleep. Her right leg was extended, with her chemise hiked up to her knee, exposing the large scratched area of skin to the air so it could dry out. Sheets of paper were spread out over the bed and her pencil had fallen to the floor. Angus picked it up and carefully gathered up the pages. He went to put them back on the desk, but then decided to sit down in the armchair and read them.

They were her boarding school memories that he had encouraged her to write down. One little story told about the day when, as the schoolgirls were eating in silence, a terrible cracking sound could be heard from the ceiling. All the girls immediately looked up and saw the leg of one of the nuns sticking through the rotting ceiling boards. General hilarity ensued among the girls while the poor nun wiggled her leg back and forth, her plump calf bulging out of her white stockings, unable to free it from the hole in the ceiling.

Angus set the pages back down on his lap. Letting his

arms drop down on either side of the armchair, he leaned his head back, closed his eyes, and smiled. It was strange to think that the young woman asleep in his bed, right next to him, was that little, naive boarding school girl just a year ago. She had followed him blindly, not knowing what she was getting herself into. Angus saw her as his traveling companion, as his equal. But every time he ran across one of her short stories, he realized that she was barely more than a little girl compared to him. When it came to his nightingale, there was a huge contrast between her intellect and her innocence.

In the train from Naples to Rome, King reserved an entire compartment for himself and Elfie, as usual. Angus threw out any traveler who asked if the unoccupied seats were free. Elfie enjoyed traveling with Angus without having to share the compartment. It meant they could discuss things openly, admire the countryside, or sleep whenever they wanted to. But her conscience ate away at her— they were cheating and being selfish.

She casually sounded him out.

"Angus, if a person benefits from the bad behavior of another person, without actually being the one to behave badly... That's not really wrong, is it? What do you think?"

"It's worse!" he snapped, categorically.

"No, it's not! The person who benefits from the bad behavior did not cause it and in no way instigated the other person to act that way. With or without that person, the bad behavior would have happened. The person who does nothing is in no way to blame!"

"He or she is even more to blame, on the contrary! For the person who commits the reprehensible deed at least had the courage to act on his beliefs and is willing to accept the consequences of them. But the one who does nothing but benefit from them is a coward because he or she does nothing to prevent the behavior, and a hypocrite because he or she reaps the benefits without paying the price."

Elfie frowned, chewing on her lower lip.

"In other words, my dear little nightingale," added Angus with a smile, "you can enjoy our private compartment, but I hope you feel quite guilty about it!"

"You're so irritating, Angus!"

"Here is the next subject for you to ponder: how to reconcile bad behavior with a good conscience."

"That would bore me to death! It sounds like a morality lesson!"

"Not so fast! Timothy would be delighted to see you chuck your conscience out the window!"

"That's not what I'm doing!"

Vecchie Rovine Castle

To get to Lady Graciosa's Vecchie Rovine Castle, they headed west from Florence. Their horse-drawn carriage crossed immense fertile plains. The wheat, tinged with gold from the setting sun, was rippling like a silk skirt in the light breeze, studded with crimson poppies that looked like rubies strewn casually over the field by an insouciant goddess of antiquity. Then, the enchanting village of Incantevole could be seen from afar, tucked against the side of a hill, a patch of ocher against the dark green forest. They hugged the shores of a lake whose smooth waters reflected the incomparable blue of the Italian sky and then climbed up toward the village.

A paved, private path lined with cypress trees led to the castle. Between each cypress stood a granite column topped with a white marble Renaissance statue of a god or goddess — rounded women and athletic men— each human body expressing divine perfection.

Decorated in earthy pink pebbledash and featuring a central covered gallery, the castle was nestled on the edge of an enchanted forest. The warmth of the sun on the south walls and the cool shadows from the forest to the north were locked in a daily contest where neither could ever claim victory. A cypress tree stood in each corner of the square courtyard that held a formal French garden with rows of glistening emerald green bushes trimmed into geometric shapes. Their sharp angles were softened by the climbing rose bushes in shades of pink and powdered cream, blooming in wild abandon along the walls of the castle and winding all the way up to the balcony of the gallery.

To Elfie, the Vecchie Rovine Castle seemed like poetry in its purest form, the idyllic background for Romeo's romance with his Juliette. She secretly wondered why the name meant *old ruins*, but then forgot about it.

Lady Graciosa told them that César de Beaumont had made a detour from Florence to her place in the hopes of seeing King there, since he knew that King was traveling in Italy. César had waited for him for two days, but then had to return to London by way of Paris.

After getting her new guests settled into their shared suite of rooms, the Countess offered to give Elfie a little tour of the castle and its gardens in the company of the other ladies who were already present. It would be a tour and an afternoon walk all at once and Graciosa's only physical exercise of the day.

Behind the castle was a labyrinth of adorable little gardens, each one enclosed by various types of hedges where you could enjoy a welcome break after walking a few yards. Elfie lost count of the little stone benches tucked into the flowering hedges, and the wrought iron gazebos covered in winding yellow roses that would be perfect for amorous confidences. Further away, a romantic wooden swing was hanging from the sturdy branch of an umbrella pine.

The ladies, each holding her parasol, emerged into a clearing to find Graciosa's bronze aviary. Covered by a pergola of gray stones, weathered with time, half invaded by a voracious mauve wisteria, the aviary sheltered dozens of birds from the sun. The sound of all these birds singing overwhelmed her Ladyship's little entourage. Birds were Graciosa's passion, and she had them brought to her from the four corners of the world.

Back in their rooms, Elfie told Angus about her walk, and especially about the birdcage.

"Have you seen the latest bird that Graciosa has brought in from France, for its unrivaled singing ability?" asked Angus.

"No, she didn't mention that one."

"It's you, nightingale! Now that she's got you trapped, she'll put you in a cage and make you sing whenever it tickles her fancy."

"That's not funny, Angus."

The next evening, in the drawing room, Elfie was singing when a new guest made his entrance. The man remained on the threshold, leaning casually against the frame of the open double doors, gazing at Elfie. Angus was right— when this man looked at her, she felt like one of Graciosa's exotic birds.

Now and then she looked over shyly at the newcomer. He was smiling, his blood red lips slightly open, showing his white teeth, including rather pointy incisors, like the fangs of a young fox. He ran his hand through his hair, which was as thick as his sister Graciosa's, but auburn, thus revealing his forehead and his striking eyes with large black pupils and irises shining like amber in the light of the candelabra.

Elfie tried in vain to critique his appearance and find some fault in it, but she found him to be perfect. He was her prince. That was her truth. Even if the exact opposite was mathematically proven to her, she would not have been capable of believing it. She was happy; therefore it was true. Her dream of love was there, right before her eyes, and very real. Not in America like Oscar Delany whom Elfie often thought of, even though she knew that it was an illusion to dream of a man separated from her by an ocean. Whereas Volpe of Vecchie Rovine, Graciosa's younger brother, was here, within her reach. That evening, he won her over with the sweet, seductive words that Elfie was longing to hear, until Angus came to get her and tell her authoritatively that it was time to retire to their rooms.

At the top of the stairs, out of eyesight, Elfie testily pulled her arm away from Angus.

"What is it?" he asked.

"So, now you're the one who gets to decide what time I have to retire for the night?"

He opened the door to their room and she went in.

"Oh, there wasn't anyone interesting there tonight, Elfie. We won't miss anything by getting to sleep early. Tomorrow there will be new guests..."

"And what if the guests suited me just fine tonight?" she interrupted him.

"By guests, you mean Volpe?"

She put an end to the conversation by saying, "I'm ringing Doreen to come undress me."

"Watch out for that man, little nightingale."

"It's fine, I know exactly what I'm doing. Try to uphold your end of our bargain, Angus!"

"What do you mean?"

"I... I have the right to act as I please."

"Absolutely. I'm only warning you."

"Imagine that! It's funny how, as if by chance, my choices are never the right ones!"

Angus smiled at Elfie's reference.

"You didn't really think that Wanton…"

She blushed. "That is none of your business, sir!"

"Yes, it is! I have no desire to pick up the pieces after certain men tear you apart. I've never done the cleaning up and I don't intend to start now."

"I'm not as innocent as you think!"

Angus smiled and leaned a little closer. "Tell me, How close did Wanton get to you?"

Seeing that Elfie was upset, he went back to being serious.

"I don't think you have fully understood who Timothy is. How can I explain him to you? Whereas you are a child of Adam and Eve… do you remember them?"

"Oh, come on, that's enough!"

"Well, Wanton is a descendant of the tempter, you see? The serpent who gave the apple to that poor innocent Eve."

"You always say mean things about people who aren't here!"

"Wanton would find this portrait to be very flattering, Elfie. He knows perfectly well what I think of him. Don't you think he already does enough gallivanting around? Don't try to make me believe that that's what you want, seeing as you are the type to wait for love with a capital L?"

"You were right, downstairs: I am tired. But tomorrow, I'll be in fine form and I'll speak to whomever I please."

"Volpe is not a wise choice," Angus insisted.

Doreen knocked at the door.

"You know what's not wise, Angus— listening to advice from a man who goes out every night no matter what city he's in, no matter what country he happens to be in at the time… Come in, Doreen!"

The two women went into the bedroom and shut the door behind them, leaving King alone in the living room.

Doreen left. Elfie started to get into bed, but then changed her mind. She tiptoed toward the door of her bedroom that opened up to the living room she shared with Angus. She put her ear up against the keyhole and heard the scratching of his quill on paper. He was writing. She stood up, forced herself to smile, and cracked open the door. Angus lifted up the quill and turned his head to look.

"Good night, Angus?"

"Good night, Elfie," he said with a smile.

She closed the door with a sigh of relief.

EPISODE 10

The Garden Swing

A week went by during which Volpe of Vecchie Rovine never missed an opportunity to express his love to Elfie with languorous looks, hands brushing together as they went from room to room, and desperate compliments on the walks they took together when King wasn't around. Volpe told her how the jewels in the royal crown would pale in comparison to her precious green eyes, that in her wake floated the lingering scent of roses that would stir the senses of even the most holy man, that nothing came close to her melodious singing which had all but ruined him on the pleasure he used to take listening to his sister's birds sing, and that the poets who lauded the radiant ivory skin of the ideal woman had obviously never seen her.

If Elfie hadn't been so blinded by her infatuation with Volpe, she would have realized that his compliments didn't hold a candle to the poetry she liked to read. But her judgment was totally derailed by the feelings Volpe aroused in her every time he approached.

At the same time, Lady Graciosa's attitude toward Elfie evolved considerably. Although Elfie was not blessed with Graciosa's classic beauty, her features were nonetheless delicate, regular, and gracious. Her eyebrows formed a thin, distinct curve that seemed to have been drawn by a stoke of a calligraphy master's paintbrush dipped in ink and placed high above her eyelids, giving her an astonished look that contrasted with the image that men had of her based on her supposed freedom brought on by her life with Angus King. This ambiguity between the candor of her features and gestures, and the imagined depravity, stoked the imaginations of the Countess's male guests. In addition, the risqué songs Elfie had learned on the Naples waterfront made each man want to be the one who would get her to drop her mask of innocence in order to savor what was hiding behind it.

The days passed by and Graciosa felt the magnetic attraction that she had always held over her little world start to slip away in favor of her young guest. This observation did not put her in a good mood. The more her beauty became haughty and stern, the less men dared try to get close to her. She had surrounded herself with an entourage for the sole purpose of having men court her, but had gotten herself trapped in a vicious circle. Graciosa knew exactly what the relationship between Angus and Elfie was, and it vexed her to hear her male guests speculate behind closed doors about the delicious romps Miss Montesquiou must regale Mr. King with in order to have changed him so completely.

The Countess called for Volpe to visit her in her boudoir.

"My dear bother," she purred, placing her hand on his forearm. "I believe that I've noticed Miss Montesquiou is not indifferent to you?"

"You know my proclivities, dear sister. I'm in love with women in general. But that little elf, I must say, piques my curiosity," he replied thoughtfully.

"Mr. King and his protegée are going to stay for another ten days. I must admit that it's already been too long for my taste. Birds are pretty when they're in their cages, but this little nightingale flying about freely overshadows me. On the other hand, I can't kick them out. That would not be proper."

"What are you getting at?" asked Volpe, squinting his eyes like a fox lying in wait. "You have always expressly asked me to leave your guests alone when they are young women."

"This is different. If by chance you fancy sinking your teeth into a bird, don't feel obligated to ask my permission."

Volpe smiled, showing all his pointy teeth. Only too happy that his plans would soon be realized, he refrained from pointing out nastily to his sister that, if she felt threatened by Elfie, it was because she knew she was getting older. Instead, he smiled at her. A smile that Graciosa returned, thinking that they were on the same wavelength. But Volpe was only thinking how lucky men were to age slower than women, that crow's feet on a man's eyes only added to his charm rather than branding him as past his prime.

One evening, Angus announced to Elfie that they would be going to Florence for two days. He wanted to meet up with a friend who was passing through that city.

"Oh, please, Angus, let's stay! It's so wonderful here."

"It'll only be for two or three days, Elfie."

"You won't need me, will you? I'm your alibi every day of the year; might I be entitled to a few days off, too, like any other employee?"

"...Why not? I suppose your dear Graciosa would be delighted to keep her singing bird around."

"You're jealous because she likes me!" she said smugly.

"The Countess loves no one but herself."

"She doesn't deserve your criticisms. She's so beautiful!"

"That should be the least of one's qualities, but in her case, it's her only one. She has you wrapped around her little finger, hasn't she? You're like a moth drawn to her flame. How can someone as intelligent as you are be so blind?"

"I'm not as intelligent as you say, and beauty counts for more in a woman."

"Dear God," exclaimed Angus, throwing his hands in the air, "if you exist, grant that I be struck deaf here and now!"

"Don't try to make me believe that you don't think so too, Angus. You assured me at Lord Wanton's that I was pretty. What's more, you declared that you liked to surround yourself with beautiful things and that I was one of them. Don't deny it."

"It was your voice that I liked when I first met you. And you happen to be pretty, which doesn't hurt, but..."

"Just say it," she interrupted, "if I had been ugly, you

wouldn't have even looked at me and certainly wouldn't have listened to me in the same way, right, Angus? You're a liar if you claim that you would have offered me your deal if I didn't have the face that I have."

"I don't deny that your pretty face weighed in your favor. But I kept you on afterwards because of your mind… You win. I'll let you stay here for a few days without me, just so I don't have to listen to your blathering. And then I'm coming back and taking you out of this idle and pointless paradise."

Elfie never took afternoon naps. She could never understand why the Countess and her retinue were always in such need of rest. They didn't get up before noon, so how could they go back to bed so soon afterwards, when their activities were limited to getting dressed and undressed several times a day, in order to be properly attired for the different times of day, and to endlessly discuss trivialities in the drawing room?

Angus had left the previous morning. In the afternoon, Elfie was strolling toward the aviary to see the birds when, out from the woods came Volpe, who offered to keep her company on her walk. They walked along the edge of the woods and came upon a garden swing hanging from an umbrella pine. Volpe offered to push her on the swing and she accepted. To the devil with Angus's warnings! What did he know about love? He was as fickle as his friend Lord Wanton. Whereas Volpe loved her…

It didn't take much to go from swinging to kissing. Volpe declared that he didn't want to upset her feelings and was happy to keep this little secret between the two of them. He asked Elfie to come meet him under this same tree the next day. Then he let her return to the castle by herself.

Elfie was on cloud nine the rest of the evening.

EPISODE 11

Modesty's Last Stand

Elfie and Volpe had a tree. Their tree. She took true delight in this secret. No one knew what was happening in her mind, in her heart. Indeed, the women and men in the drawing room were far from feeling this happiness that flooded her body and heart. It gave her a feeling of superiority— she had a unique and marvelous secret that no one else knew about. She sang for Volpe alone that night, glancing discreetly at him from time to time, and sharing a knowing look.

She didn't read or write, but went straight to bed, leaving her bedroom window open to the warm night air. She heard a knock on the window pane. Elfie jumped out of bed in alarm and was startled when she saw a man. Volpe had appeared at the window, his hands on the window sill, his body leaning into the room while the rest of his body remained outside. It seemed a rather precarious position, fifteen feet up from the ground with only the tips of his shoes wedged into a crevice between two stones in the wall to keep him from falling. Volpe asked for nothing but a kiss before he climbed down, or else he would die of love. Elfie smiled at her Romeo, leaned slightly toward Volpe's face, hesitated, and then kissed him. He smiled too, showing his teeth in a strange way, and then without another word, climbed down the way he had come up.

Elfie had found her Romeo. Where else could she have found him but in Italy, the country of sun and passion?

The following day, Volpe arrived at their umbrella pine at the same time as Elfie did. In her room before leaving, she had fussed at length over which dress to wear to this first romantic tryst of her life. She had at last decided on a light, white muslin dress dotted with little red flowers and delicate garlands of pale green leaves, with a colorful, wide silk ribbon tied around her narrow waist.

Overflowing with obvious passion, Volpe rushed toward her, took her by the hand, and led her toward the forest.

"The castle as you know it," he explained, "dates from the Renaissance. It was built not far from the ruins of an ancient residence that still exist."

They walked into the deep shadows of the tall trees. Elfie

held her skirts tight against her legs with her free hand as she followed Volpe, who was clearing the way by pushing aside the branches and brambles that had overgrown the path.

They walked along for about fifteen minutes, making their way through the undergrowth. Volpe helped Elfie as best he could as she held on to her wide-brimmed summer hat. At times he held back low branches and ferns with one hand for her to pass by, other times he held her skirts against her legs so she wouldn't tear them. Elfie felt a thrill when she felt Volpe's hand on her thighs through her petticoats. They came across a clearing. There, stone columns stood upon pedestals holding ancient statues that had withstood the passage of time. Together, they caressed the cold yet smooth marble of Venus's belly that was ever so rounded just below her navel. They ran their hands over the curve of her hips that led to her marble bottom.

They went beyond the ruins, which were mostly hidden under fragrant thyme covered in little purple flowers. They plunged deeper into the abundant foliage and arrived at a fountain. Up against an ancient wall, a granite basin held clear, fresh water from a nearby spring. Seated on the edge of the basin was a chubby stone cherub, with a mischievous yet friendly smile, dipping his little hand into the water since the dawn of time.

Volpe took a drink straight from the stream of clear water that continuously spurted out of the wall, and then offered some to Elfie in his cupped hands.

"Drink, my friend. This water has been blessed by Cupid for more than two thousand years."

She couldn't resist. She had read poetry and believed that she was finally living it, in this forest— it was overwhelming.

Volpe took Elfie to a little nest of soft grass next to a wall that must have been the inner wall of a drawing room or a boudoir where the faded mosaics, in warm tones of ocher and pink, depicted beautiful gods and carefree goddesses in the throes of passion. He made her promise to never reveal his secret hideaway.

Volpe kissed her as he unfastened her bodice, sending a thrill through her body. Within her, the burning desires of a flesh and blood woman and the prudish, flower-strewn dreams of a boarding school girl mingled together. Volpe removed her bodice and let it drop to the ground. Liberated from this tight-fitting garment, her small round breasts were in full bloom under her chemise.

He murmured, "You are so beautiful and I love you so much! Isn't that an ideal combination?"

"Yes... maybe..."

"My friend, I no longer know myself, I am lost. Your charms dazzle my thoughts. You are more beautiful than Venus, my statue of flesh and blood. Let me look at you, admire you," he said, pulling her chemise down over her corset to reveal her bosom. "Oh, divine creature! All the sculptors of antiquity must be turning over in their graves because they didn't have you as a model!"

"That's nonsense, Mr. Volpe!"

"I always speak the truth when it comes to love!" he proclaimed, kissing her pink breasts and unlacing her corset, which ended up on the ground along with her bodice. "All the gods would have fought to the death over you."

Volpe leaned over Elfie, who let him explore her skin. After all, there was no harm in this little game, there were no lasting consequences. He kissed her so much that it made her head spin, until she felt his hand between her thighs, under her petticoats. She jumped up all at once.

"That's it, that's enough!" she exclaimed naively, pulling her chemise up over her chest.

"Oh, no! You unfeeling creature," cried Volpe, looking at her with puppy dog eyes as if he were about to cry. "I've been professing my love to you for days and you ride roughshod over it. I'm putting all my love at the mercy of your kind heart and you reject it?"

"No, I don't!" she protested, sitting back down next to Volpe.

"I must confess something to you. From the night I first saw you, divine apparition, I have been besotted with you. It keeps me up at night. I've seen in your beautiful eyes our shared desire to unite ourselves in the most powerful, most pure love that has ever existed."

"Really?"

"And these pretty little feet that I have not even been able to kiss yet, as one should when one loves as much as I love you. At least let me kiss your precious little feet!"

"Does it mean that much to you?" she asked, all trace of resistance gone from her voice.

"Oh, yes! Thank you," he said, gently placing her feet on his lap and removing her little embroidered shoes one at a time. "How can a human being possibly stand on such petite, such delicate little feet? May I find out?" he asked, putting his request into action by expertly untying the ribbon that held her stocking in place above her knee. "You are the queen of my heart."

I am the queen of his heart, Elfie repeated to herself. *Volpe loves me and he is Graciosa's brother. I'll be Lord Wanton's sister-in-law. Then I'll no longer visit Lord Wanton as Angus's alibi, but as Timothy's equal, and he'll be proud of me. I will truly be part of his world and he will hold me in esteem.*

His face buried in Elfie's white feet, Volpe savored his good fortune with jaded indifference. He was irresistible and no innocent young lady had ever dared to entertain the thought that it was possible to not succumb to his charm. He took his time gently kissing Elfie's little feet and her shapely calves. He liked to relish the promise of discovering a new, tender, soft body.

However, Elfie, trembling under his caress, withdrew.

"It's true that I love you, but why don't we wait until…"

"But I love you! I'd rather die than put off our love for another minute. You can not delay love, Elfie. You might as well try to put off the sunrise. Is that possible, my beloved?"

"No, of course not…"

"Then why make me wait, when our love is stronger than Romeo and Juliette's love?"

At those two names, Volpe knew from Elfie's slight tremble that he had secured his victory.

"If you make me wait, my love," he added, "my life will be nothing but an endless night."

Volpe kissed Elfie's feet and ankles… Then, with an experienced hand, he lifted up her skirt, and, as her modesty's last stand fell to his caresses, the maiden's firm, smooth thighs opened up as she surrendered to his kisses…

EPISODE 12

Going Separate Ways

Every afternoon, Elfie and Volpe met under the umbrella pine and ran off toward their secret nest deep within the enchanted forest. Elfie thought that her whole life would be as sweet as those afternoons. To thank this man whom she loved, this man who had made her into a woman, Elfie showered Volpe with caresses, affection, and whispered sweet nothings.

"I am your servant, my love," she swooned, giving in to his every desire.

"How I love you," he replied, caressing her hair and savoring the pleasure of being seen as a lord with full powers.

And how he did love her innocent and submissive ways.

Each night, in her room, Elfie found either a bouquet of flowers or a basket of candied fruit that Volpe had sent to her, accompanied by four lines of flattering poetry written on scented paper.

On the fourth day, as Volpe helped her to refasten her bodice, Elfie asked, "Volpe? Do you think that the Countess will be happy to learn that she and I will become sisters-in-law?"

"I'm sure she will," he replied breezily, "but..."

Here we are, he thought, *She's broken the spell. Why do women always return to reality too soon?"*

"...let me find the right moment to tell her the news," he said, fiddling testily with her dress. "Why won't this hook fit....?"

Elfie remained silent.

"Perhaps," he continued carefully, "it would be better if you speak to King about it before we mention it to anyone else, my beloved? It seems to me that it involves him first and foremost."

"Yes, you're right. He deserves to be the first to know."

Later that afternoon, after his rendezvous with Elfie, Volpe went to see his sister in her room. Graciosa had finally woken up from her nap, but had not gotten out of bed yet. Her lady's maid suggested dress after dress in the hopes of finding one that the Countess would agree to wear for the late afternoon. Reclining on her bed in a flattering position, propped up on a thousand lacy pillows, she mustered enough energy to indicate her preferences to her lady's maid with a point of her finger.

"Volpe, my dear little brother, to what do I owe the honor? You're looking quite put out."

"Indeed, I'm bored," he said, stretching out casually on the bed next to his sister.

"You've been so full of energy and ardor these past few days."

"That's true. I'm full of enthusiasm when I have a new conquest in my sights, a new heart to subdue. You see, Graciosa, right now I feel like a military general and consummate tactician who is positioning his troops: I've sent love letter, flowers, and fruit, not too much, not too little. When the enemy least expects it, I bestow a compliment, I refrain from a caress, I give a wink— just to keep her on her toes and make it so she can think of nothing but me. Just as Napoleon wanted every country at his feet, I want every woman at mine."

"Correction, Volpe, you want only the young and pretty women."

"You are right. I thank you for this correction, which is entirely to my credit," he said with a smile that revealed his canines.

"So, why this weary look?"

"What I love, Graciosa, is to wrap a little heart around my finger and hold a great virtue in my arms. But nowadays, I find that the fortresses are no longer all that difficult to take. The conquest is less of a challenge. The battle is brief and the victory is assured from the outset. It's much less fun!"

"Poor dear! As long as I can remember, you have always been hard to satisfy."

"Think what you wish, big sister!" replied Volpe with a pout. "In any case, once the enemy's surrender is assured, what's left? Nothing. A thigh, even a shapely one, no matter how plump, fair, and smooth it is, is nevertheless the exact same tomorrow as it was yesterday. What's the interest in that? Once you've taken the tour, you're back to where you started," he frowned, annoyed at his own misfortune.

"I have had the same thoughts for ages, only about men! Volpe... it seems to me that you tire of them more and more quickly."

"It seems to me that it's the women who take things too seriously more and more quickly. The moment they let you into their inner sanctum, they start talking about "always" and "forever"... no, really, I'm tired of it!"

The next day, there were no jaunts through the forest, no admiring the statues of antiquity. Volpe went straight to the point. He undressed Elfie and put her clothes back on almost without saying a word.

On the way back, he let her drink alone at the fountain for the first time, without cupping the water in his hands for her. Elfie noticed the change, but told herself that it was the thought of having to face King's return that was bothering Volpe. She understood. The night before, she hadn't stopped worrying about how she was going to break the news to Angus that she was going to leave him.

The following day, Mr. King had still not reappeared. Volpe let Elfie unfasten her own bodice and didn't wait for her to remove her corset or her petticoats. His love couldn't wait, he told her. They returned to the castle separately, as usual.

How could she have known that Volpe of Vecchie Rovine was nothing but a playboy? That she was easy prey for a man such as him: cunning, manipulative, and experienced. Of course Elfie was intelligent and was figuring things out as best she could, but her sheltered education had in no way prepared her to face the type of man that Graciosa's brother was.

Volpe didn't appear for the rest of the evening, and no bouquet of flowers awaited Elfie in her room. She hardly slept at all and when she did, it was fitful. She couldn't stop thinking back over every detail of her last two meetings with Volpe. Had she said or done something that had annoyed him, or even hurt him? Had she just imagined that the Count of Vecchi Rovine had become slightly indifferent, or was this feeling grounded in fact? Had she smiled enough? Been attentive enough to his desires? Where and when had she made her mistake?

Volpe did not show up the next day at lunch either. As none of the other guests brought it up, Elfie didn't dare question the Countess about it, for fear of betraying their secret. The hours leading up to time of their meeting under the umbrella pine seemed like centuries to Elfie.

Finally, once she was sure that everyone had retired to their own rooms, Elfie left the castle at an unhurried pace. Once out of sight from the castle, she ran toward the pine tree, her heart racing. No one was there. She sat down on the swing. She waited for more than an hour, and then went back, dejected.

All at once, she missed Angus. She paced back and forth in their little living room, then sat down at the desk where Angus had left a few pages covered in black ink from his tiny, compact writing. She took one of Angus's jackets out of the wardrobe and laid down on the sofa, completely distraught, holding the jacket in her arms and pulling it up to her nose to smell it. Her gaze fell on the last bouquet of flowers that Volpe had sent.

Suddenly, she got up, a big smile on her face, and threw the jacket onto the couch. Of course! Why hadn't she thought of it earlier? Volpe was in Florence! He must have gone there to find King and spare her the difficult task of breaking the news to him that she would no longer be staying with him! Volpe was going to surprise her by taking care of their future together. She wasn't used to it with Angus, but Volpe was a thoughtful and sensitive man. He had merely been distracted the day before by the thought of meeting with King. Once again on cloud nine, she rang for Doreen to come help her dress for the evening.

After dinner, Elfie sang Rossini's *La Danza* with renewed confidence, blissfully unaware of Graciosa's frown of surprise at her astonishingly good mood. But, a thousand miles from guessing what the Countess already knew, Elfie was glowing and more attractive than ever. They were leaving the music room when she heard some people exclaim:

"Mr. King, you have returned at last!"

Elfie got up on her tiptoes, but had to wait for the crowd around double doors to disperse before she saw Angus enter after shaking hands with the guests who were leaving. Elfie smiled at him sincerely. She really had missed him a lot. She looked for Volpe behind him and was a little disappointed not to see him there.

"Well, nightingale, what a welcome! You don't seem very happy to see me!"

"Oh, of course I am!"

She held out her hands, but Angus took her by the waist and lifted her up to kiss her on the forehead.

"Please, Angus, show a little restraint, I'm not a child anymore!"

"Oh, really? And since when?" he asked unwittingly.

Elfie was flustered. "I spoke without thinking... I didn't mean anything by it!"

"Neither did I!" he said, intrigued. "Come on, let's go upstairs. I'm exhausted. Tell me about what you read this week, my little alibi."

Elfie followed him reluctantly. What did he know? What was she going to tell him? What had Volpe told him?"

While Angus freshened up in their water closet with the door cracked opened, he spoke to Elfie who was sitting on the sofa in the living room.

"So, tell me, did you try to read Thomas Moore's poetry?"

"No, I didn't have the time."

"Not even *The Last Rose of Summer*?"

"What rose? The rose bushes are still in full bloom," she said distractedly.

Angus appeared, bare-chested, drying off his neck. All the delicious Italian pasta and wine had really filled out his stomach, Elfie noticed.

"So, what did you read then, nightingale?"

"What is this, an interrogation?"

He sat down across from her, in an armchair.

"What's gotten in to you?"

"I'm going to ring for Doreen; it's been a long evening. And put a shirt on, Angus!"

"You seem different, nightingale. Yes, you've changed."

"I grew up, believe it or not! You'll have to get used to it."

She got up and strode past him, silent and haughty above the rustling of her pink silk skirt. Angus grabbed her wrist and stood up, his massive frame towering over her.

"Don't be so selfish!" he sang out gleefully. "Tell me about your adventures. Who gave you this new sense of confidence?"

"No one did. It's none of your business!"

"As you wish. What a treat it is to come back and find you in such a good mood! Have I told you about the series of classes and conferences that I've agreed to do in the United States, this winter?"

"I don't believe you have."

"Well, it's been confirmed! In two days, we'll take the train to Genoa, then on to London via Paris, a short stop in Ireland, and then off to New York."

"What? In two day? But you never said anything about this! I won't be able to come."

"Graciosa likes you, but she's not going to keep you around forever."

"I... Angus, listen. Come sit near me, please."

He obeyed, the vertical crease on his forehead furrowing as he began to be concerned.

"Here goes," said Elfie calmly. "You know, our deal... it can't last forever. I thank you for taking me in. I will be eternally grateful for that. But now, I'm going to have to let you go on your own to America."

"Why?"

"It's just that I..."

"Why?"

"I am loved by a man."

"I suspected that you were no longer the same. And what about you, do you love him?"

"Why... yes, of course!"

"Why did you hesitate then?"

"I didn't hesitate!"

"Who is it?"

"How is that any of your business?"

"A fleeting romance is one thing, but if you intend to spend your life with this man— seeing as we have lived together for months now— I thought you would have shared this news with me more readily and with more enthusiasm. But if you think I should be in the dark until I read about your marriage in the gossip columns, that's your choice!" he retorted coldly.

"It's just that… you don't like this man."

"At least it's not Volpe!" he laughed dismissively.

Elfie stood up nervously.

"I'm ringing for Doreen."

"What? You're kidding me! It can't be him, I saw him in Florence this morning!"

"There, you see? What did he tell you?"

"He neither saw me nor spoke to me. I happened to see him leaving his current favorite mistress's place, Rosa… Rosa… I forget her last name."

"You are mistaken, Mr. King!" cried Elfie, a dagger in her heart.

"Not at all. Tell me it's not him!"

"It is him and he loves me!"

"How do you know he does?"

"He told me so."

"I saw him, Elfie. Believe me, I'm not the only one who saw him."

"Fine, so what if you did. Perhaps he went there discreetly to tell that woman that is was over with her? Of course, that must be it."

"Or perhaps he went there discreetly to fuck her?"

"You are vulgar!"

"I'm realistic, and you are not. When did he leave?"

"Yesterday afternoon."

"And what did he tell you before he left?"

Elfie, on the verge of tears, her chin trembling, but holding back from breaking down completely, went to ring for Doreen.

"This is none of your business, Angus. You wouldn't understand. He'll be here tomorrow, you'll see!"

"Nightingale, he won't be back."

"Why are you so mean?"

"You won't listen to reason, will you?" he asked gently.

There was a knock at the door.

"Come in, Doreen!"

"You're just in time, Doreen," said Angus to the lady's maid. "We're leaving tomorrow. You can pack my trunk later, but start packing Mademoiselle's trunk immediately."

"Very well, sir."

Doreen went into the bedroom, pulled the trunk out of the closet, opened it up, and started to empty the shelves of the wardrobe. Quietly, Elfie closed the bedroom door behind Doreen, and, in the living room, whispered so her lady's maid couldn't hear, "I'm not leaving with you, Angus!"

EPISODE 13

Murky Waters

In the living room, Elfie took a deep breath and said more calmly, "I'm waiting for Volpe. He's going to return. Please, Angus, you must understand."

"Volpe has already seduced more than a hundred innocent young ladies just like you, if not more than that!"

"There you go again saying mean things about those who are absent!"

"But open your eyes! I suppose no one else knows that you were seeing each other this past week?"

"…?"

"Elfie, the only thing that has happened here, is that he pounced on you the moment I had my back turned, and he left as soon as heard I was returning."

"I hate you! You make everything dirty! Just because you lead a disparate life… Everyone is not like you, Angus! There are men who find that loving one person is enough. I don't want to hear any more!"

Elfie abruptly opened the bedroom door to see Doreen filling the trunk.

"Put my things back, Doreen, please! We are staying."

The lady's maid stopped in mid-motion, not knowing what to do. Elfie took the corset that she held in her hands and put it back into the dresser.

"Come now, do as I say, please!"

"Doreen," King said calmly from the doorway. "Pack the trunks like I asked you to."

"Mademoiselle?" the lady's maid asked Elfie.

"Don't forget you pays your wages, Doreen," was King's parting shot as he left the bedroom.

"I'm sorry, mademoiselle," said the lady's maid, putting the corset into the trunk once again.

Elfie followed Angus.

"So, that's it? You have the money, so you get to decide about my life? I thought you were different, but you are like them, like my father, like d'Orvigny!"

"That's enough!"

"You're even worse because you led me to believe the opposite!"

Angus was going to yell at her to shut up or to stay here to wait indefinitely for her vile seducer, but Wanton's words came back to him.

Your deal is unequal and you know it. Don't hide the fact that she needs protection and that you are the only protector that she has for the time being. You are responsible for her now, whether you like it or not.

"Elfie," he continued as calmly as he could. "It's not a question of money. Are you sure of yourself? I beg of you, analyze the situation. Is there any evidence to convince you of what I'm saying? Think with your mind and not with your heart."

"…"

Her last meeting with Volpe had left Elfie with a bitter taste in her mouth and in her heart. But she resisted what Angus said in order to persuade herself that he was wrong.

"Did he leave a note explaining why he disappeared?" questioned Angus.

"No," she continued in a calm voice. "But surely he was just worried that someone might intercept it?"

"I have nothing against a romp in the hay, as you know; that is not the issue. But why would he have asked you to keep it a secret for days and days?"

"He was waiting for the right moment to tell his sister…?"

"In what way does it concern the gracious Countess? Volpe need not ask her opinion."

"We thought it would be best to speak to you about it first," persisted Elfie.

"You knew the address of my hotel in Florence. Why didn't I receive any word from you, or from him?"

"…"

Elfie lowered her green eyes, squinting them into two narrow slits, as if to not see the reality in front of her.

"He hid you from everyone, my little nightingale. That's

not how an honest man in love acts."

"You said before that we would leave in two days," Elfie tried again. "Why move up our departure for tomorrow?"

"So I don't have to see you pine away waiting for a man who's not worth it. So your heartbreak won't be on display for Graciosa's court. And speaking of Graciosa, if she had been your friend, she would have warned you about her brother. If there's one thing she's good at, it's not missing a single innuendo. Deep down, you know I am right."

"Why didn't the Countess warn me? It doesn't make sense. Graciosa likes me, doesn't she… ?"

"You and Timothy spent your time arm in arm, laughing together like children, even during Graciosa's stay in Old Queen Street."

"But… no…" ventured Elfie.

"You and Timothy discussed the novels he lent you right in front of Graciosa, who couldn't follow along because she never reads."

"But, Angus, Lord Wanton explained to me that it was only a marriage of convenience for both of them, and the Countess confided to me in London that the only reason she had married him was to benefit from his magnificent London pied-à-terre. I don't see how I could have… I never did anything to exclude the Countess from our conversations!"

"But you never went out of your way to discuss things that would have included her in the conversation either."

"But… what is your point?"

"Graciosa let her brother get close to you. Jealously always devours a woman's heart, Elfie."

"That's not very clever, or very fair, to make such sweeping statements," said Elfie, who did not want to give in. "It's you, Angus, who are Machiavellian, imagining such terrible things! Angus, give me a chance to prove that you're wrong. Let's not leave for another two days, please!"

King had finally run out of all his reserves of patience.

"We're leaving tomorrow, at ten o'clock in the morning! Be ready, because I'm taking you with even if you're wearing nothing but your chemise! I don't give a damn about your pathetic little romance. I'll need my alibi among the Puritans in America!" he said angrily, more irritated with himself than with Elfie. "This discussion is over!"

Angus had not protected her from Volpe. He had left Elfie alone, in the hands of that seducer. Making a deal with someone entailed a lot more than Angus had imagined. To say nothing of the fact that the night he had proposed that deal to Elfie, he hadn't for one moment considered the consequences. He, being the egoist that he was, had only seen her as an unassailable alibi for himself. Had he, also, taken advantage of her in a way? Was he any better than Volpe? Angus and Elfie had been living together for... nine months now, he realized in amazement. Nine months, what an interesting amount of time. He stopped himself right there in his thoughts, not wanting to come to the conclusion that was staring him in the face: he had grown attached to his alibi.

In her bedroom, Elfie let Doreen help her get undressed, and then ignored her. Doreen continued packing the trunk. When she determined that she had made enough progress for the night, seeing as Elfie had gone to bed and had blown out the lamp, Doreen got ready to retire. Before she left, suspecting that her mistress was not yet sleeping, she approached the bed and whispered:

"Mademoiselle, I'm packing your trunks because Mr. King asked me to, but also because I think he's right about His Lordship, the Count of Vecchie Rovine... I'm sorry, mademoiselle."

No secret was unknown to a lady's maid. Elfie wasn't at all angry with Doreen for having chosen to obey the one who paid her wages. Hadn't she done the same thing herself when she had to decide between the street or his financial protection?

How could Volpe leave her without any news for... Elfie counted, thirty-two hours now? Is this what she had been reduced to? Counting the hours on her fingers? No, Angus was wrong, Doreen was wrong. Volpe would come back. But a tiny voice, which she had been suppressing since yesterday, infiltrated her thoughts.

Day after day, Volpe's attentions had waned until they had finally disappeared on the last afternoon. But no! He had not grown weary, she must have faith. Anyone can have worries or fickle moods, no man is perfect.

Yes, but... was Angus right after all? Volpe had seduced her only after King had left and then had disappeared before he came back. But then, that might just be a coincidence, right?

Elfie fell asleep just before dawn. Her dreams were alive with magnificent gods and goddess from antiquity, statues of polished white marble, smooth to the touch, remnants of fairy tale castles, age-old trees, decadent gods dancing in dubious clearings, statues whose broken-off limbs left jagged marble edges, stone ruins eroded by time, brambles that tore at her skirt, ancient, twisted, gnarled trees that swallowed her up into their cavernous trunks, and the crafty Volpe, who turned into a fox with yellow eyes and returned to the murky forest after having devoured a bird escaped from the aviary, a nightingale who would never sing again... Elfie awoke with a start, covered in sweat. Even the nights in this land were too hot!

The day dawned pink and mauve. Elfie went to the window and smiled as she thought of her Romeo's appearance a week earlier. Angus was completely mistaken! This nightmare was entirely his fault. King was the only man who wanted to keep his nightingale caged up. She was a woman, a desired and beloved woman. She wasn't going to give up over a small obstacle, was she? Devoted lovers always face them, but she and Volpe would triumph over them. She tiptoed out of the room in her bare feet and settled down at the desk to write a letter.

At ten o'clock that morning, the author and his alibi asked for an audience in Graciosa's rooms to say their goodbyes. The Countess received them in a carefully designed mise-en-scene. In an elegant state of undress, her artfully undone hair cascaded across the pillows.

"You're leaving us so soon, friends?" she said.

"Dear Countess," said King, "My first conference in New York is in October and we must go to Ireland before that. You can see that we have no time to lose."

"The main thing is that you thoroughly enjoyed yourselves during your stay here," she said, looking Elfie right in the eyes.

"Your Ladyship," said Elfie with a smile, glad that her education had taught her such complete self-control. "We have had a wonderful time."

"Oh!" she exclaimed, "This is my least favorite season. It started with my dear brother and now everyone is leaving. You will miss nothing by leaving now— Volpe was the first to go and won't be returning any time soon. I received a note from him this morning saying that he was off to Rome. My brother is mysterious. But I know him, there's a woman behind this, I'm sure of it. What a rascal! But he's fun to be around, isn't he, mademoiselle?" persisted

Graciosa with feigned innocence.

"That is true," Elfie agreed, still smiling, but on the verge of fainting. "Your brother always has a kind word to please the ladies in the drawing room, Your Ladyship."

Angus was impressed with Elfie's self-control and added:

"Graciosa, we have a long road ahead of us. Thank you for your hospitality. Perhaps we will meet again in London, at Lord Wanton's one of these days?" he said, kissing her hand.

Climbing into the carriage, Elfie realized that Angus had been right all along. Like an idiot, she had let herself be seduced by a worthless man. And to think that this very morning, she had still hoped it wasn't like that. But Volpe was already far away, and was perhaps already eyeing his next victim?

Doreen climbed up on to the front bench next to the driver and the horses set off.

"Wait, Angus!" cried Elfie. "I forgot something in my room."

From his jacket pocket, King took out the letter Elfie had written that morning to Volpe.

"This?"

Elfie, furious and humiliated, reached out her hand to grab it, but Angus slipped it back into his pocket.

"You cleaned out my room before leaving, Angus? You usually aren't so careful. Did you read it?"

"Yes. It's terrible writing. That's not the kind of prose that would have convinced your lover to rush back to you on the next train."

Sitting stiffly on the carriage bench, Elfie swallowed her humiliation. She had only one desire, and that was to lash out savagely at her travel companion; because he was there in front of her and she had no one else to vent her rage on. Instead, with a jerk, she forced her hands into a ladylike position on her lap, breathing raggedly through her nose.

They reached the plains. The wheat has been harvested, and the fields were now nothing but a black expanse of earth bristling with dry, gray straw stubble. Barefooted children wearing rough work smocks were gleaning the remaining ears of wheat that still lay scattered on the ground. The black cypress trees along the edge of the roads barred the sky like the upraised lances of soldiers going off to war. *This country is but the décor of a theater where the worst farces in the world are played out!* though Elfie. The frescoes in the churches, the sculptures in the museums, the beautiful, indolent Italian women, the fruit that melted in your mouth— all that was nothing but an intricate trap set to seduce you and then inexorably close down upon you. Elfie lowered her eyes, not wanting to see anything more until after they had crossed the border out of Italy.

Their path took them back along the shores of the lake. When had she seen the sky's reflection in it? The water was murky and black. Angus lowered the side window, took out the letter from his pocket, tore it up into a thousand pieces, and threw them toward the lake. She watched furtively as the little scraps of paper telling the story of her love were submerged into the deep water.

Elfie tried to concentrate on the folds of her skirt, on the shape of her leather gloves. Everything was jumbled up inside her head in an infernal turmoil. She felt like she was sinking into the black lake water, just like the scraps of paper. She was suffocating. She was going to die in this carriage before anyone had ever loved her. Nine months earlier she had left her family. She remembered what she had said to Angus in that hansom cab as they headed into Paris:

"I could disappear off the face of the earth today, and no trace of my passage would remain."

What had changed since then? She had experienced love. No, it wasn't love. She didn't even know what to call what she had done, if it wasn't love. How could she have been so deceived? Volpe had lied. But was he alone guilty? Hadn't she seen things that didn't exist, just because she had wanted so much to believe them? Because she longed so desperately for romance? She leaned over, stuck her feet out from under her skirt and studied them. So nothing he had said was true, then? Were her feet adorable? Elfie removed her gloves and examined her hands next: were they slender and white enough? They were not as attractively plump as artists usually painted them. Was her bosom full enough to hold a man's interest? Was it her body that had driven Volpe away? Wasn't she pretty enough to be loved by a man? What was the point of even wondering? No man would ever want her now.

EPISODE 14

To the Old Ruins

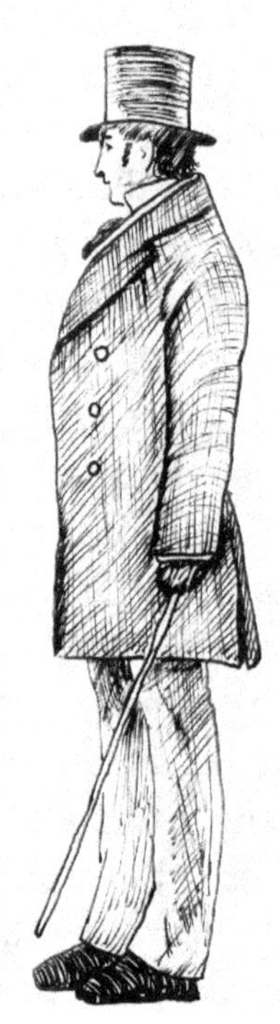

In Genoa, they had an hour to kill before their connecting train. Angus suggested a little walk through the old village to stretch their legs, but Elfie refused on the pretext of not wanting to miss their train. She didn't even want to step outside the railway station to admire its columns and caryatids.

Doreen had found a porter to collect their trunks and

hand bags, and was chatting with him on the platform. Doreen found it easy to converse with everyone. Elfie watched her lady's mad. She really was fond of her. Doreen was kind, hard-working, and blessed with common sense that Elfie lacked. She realized now that Doreen had seen things that she herself had not seen. At Vecchie Rovine, she had warned her about Volpe. One day, as she was arranging the candied fruit that Volpe had sent as a present to Elfie, Doreen had pointed out:

"Sometimes, certain gifts can be poisonous."

The following day, Doreen had also let slip a comment about the flowers, but Elfie had paid no attention to it. *Yes, Elfie said to herself, Doreen is a good woman*. She promised herself that in the future, she would be more careful with her belongings to make things easier on Doreen.

Angus sat down on a bench and took a book out of his pocket. Elfie, standing motionless on the platform, stared down at the tracks without speaking, holding her little leather travel bag in front of her with both hands.

They could hear a train approaching. Angus looked up at his alibi. Suddenly, he had a sense of foreboding:

"Elfie, come over near me, please! You're blocking the platform for other travelers."

She turned toward him indifferently and came over to stand next to the bench where he was sitting. Angus was reassured. His little nightingale didn't seem to be entertaining any irrevocable ideas. He looked at her slender silhouette, taking in her youthful profile, her childish little nose, her pink cheeks, the slightly surprised look in her eyes even as they reflected her deep disappointment in the world, and her wide forehead full of intelligence.

A train passed by without stopping, bringing with it a powerful, metallic blast of air that swept up a gust of dirt from the platform. Elfie's skirts poofed up as they were sucked toward the machine barreling past at full steam, pulling her slightly off balance.

Angus promised himself to take care of himself so that he could protect her.

They stopped over at Marseille for a night and stayed in a little hotel on Athens Boulevard, not far from the Saint Charles train station. They got only one room for the two of them, to save on costs, and a small room for Doreen. That night, Angus settled down to write at the tiny desk provided in their modest room.

Doreen helped Elfie, who thanked her and then got ready for bed by herself. She folded her petticoats and carefully hung up her skirt and bodice in the wardrobe, taking her time and trying to delay the moment when she would have to go to bed as soon as Angus finished his article and blew out the lamp. She knew that she wouldn't sleep much.

Angus, leaning over his work, heard her fussing about, moving her hand bag around, opening and closing the wardrobe, washing her face in the basin on the dressing table. He found it distracting and annoying, but for once, he didn't say anything about it to her, understanding that his nightingale's disappointment was preventing her from reading or even writing.

Elfie began to sing softly *Plaisir d'Amour*:

The joys of love are but a moment long,
The pain of love endures the whole life long.
Your eyes kissed mine, I saw the love in them shine
You brought me heaven right then when your eyes kissed mine.
My love loves me, and all thy wonders I see
The rainbow shines in my window, my love loves me

And now he's gone like a dream that fades into dawn
But the words stay locked in my heartstrings, my love loves me
The joys of love are but a moment long,
The pain of love endures the whole life long.

Angus King dipped his quill into his ink pot with a sense of confidence. If Elfie still had the courage to sing, it meant that she would get over this. He merely had to be patient, even if he wasn't very good at that. *As long as it doesn't take too long!* he couldn't help but think, like the egoist he was.

From Marseille to Lyon, they had a compartment all to themselves— there weren't very many people on the train.

"Do you want to eat something, nightingale?" he asked.

"No, thank you, Angus. Maybe later."

"It will get better."

He didn't have to say any more. Volpe had been hanging in the air between them ever since they had left Vecchie Rovine Castle.

"Nothing was true, Angus?" she asked in barely a whisper, hoping that he would not brush her off. "Was I just kidding myself?"

"Yes."

"He said he loved me, but it wasn't true?"

"No, it wasn't true. But you couldn't have known."

"But I should have. I wanted a romance so badly that I made it all up: Romeo, the enchanted forest, the secrets of the ruins. How many times had he already climbed that wall? He probably knew every handhold on it. Romeo is made up; no man risks his life or dies for a woman in real life. I thought that the marble statues and ruins were remnants of the past, but the green moss that covered them was nothing but a putrid leprosy. The old stones had crumbled without anyone caring about their history. The brambles were in no way romantic, they just tore up my skirts. Vecchie Rovine— the old ruins— it's a fitting name for that castle!"

Elfie thought about her prettiest white muslin skirt, the one with little red flowers and green leaves that she wore to that first rendezvous. That evening, Doreen had told her that the little tears in the skirt made by the brambles could not be repaired, even with the finest of needles. She would have to replace it, but her wages weren't enough for that right now. At the time, Elfie hadn't cared a bit about the tattered skirt; it was so unimportant compared to Volpe's love for her. But Volpe's love had never existed and nothing was left for her now but the expense of a new dress. *How pathetic*, she thought.

"I'm sorry, Elfie. I shouldn't have left you there. You were not ready to tell the difference between the ideal lover and the reality of a man."

"… But… Everything he said was a lie?"

"What do you mean?"

"He complimented my…"

She lowered her eyes to look at her body.

"… my hands," she whispered. "But he didn't really think so?"

"There is no doubt that he did indeed think so. Your… hands are as pretty as they come. On that subject, he was not lying. In fact, that is the reason he set his sights on you."

"How can you tell the truth from the lies?"

"With experience."

"I'm not going to have any more experiences, Angus."

"That would surprise me.

"I can assure you!"

Angus smiled, "May I dare to hope that the discovery was at least pleasurable?"

"Angus!"

"What? Perhaps it's too soon to tell you this, but sort through your memories and only keep the best ones, unless there weren't any good ones?"

"Of course there were. Oh, you're so annoying!"

"Here!" he said, handing her his notebook and a pencil. "Don't waste another precious day with regrets. Write down all the resentment you feel about him; it will help you forget all about him."

"No, I'd rather learn fencing! And beat him in a duel! Make his blood pour down his lacy silk collar and spank you soundly with the point of my blade to teach you to watch your language! ... How I miss the time when I dreamed of love. I thought it was a waste of time if it wasn't real, but those are the best moments in life, Angus, I'm sure of it."

"Remind me how old you are, again?"

"Sixteen, why?"

He smiled bemusedly.

"Oh, yes, I know! You've lived more than I have. Don't mind me, poke fun at me all you want!"

"I'm not making fun of you, Elfie. I'm only saying that as painful as it was, it was only one experience. You will have others."

"But I don't want... didn't want to have experiences. I was tricked, Angus. I would have never done... what I did, if I had known that it wasn't love."

"I don't approve one bit of the methods he used either, but there is nothing that can be done to stop that man."

"Too bad, because my heart has plenty of ideas for revenge. He poisoned me, you can't even imagine how much."

They only stopped in Paris for two days. They once again stayed at César de Beaumont's apartment while he was away in Austria. Gilbert and Francine welcomed them to Rue de Morny, and Elfie was pleased to come back to the apartment that, for her, symbolized the biggest decision of her life and her first days of freedom.

Since they had left Italy, Elfie had not written a word. On several occasions, Angus had handed her paper and pencil, but she had set them back down distractedly. He didn't say anything, but inwardly seethed. He was aware that the deplorable affair with Volpe had seriously shaken her, but he only had so much patience. He couldn't understand why she didn't do what had worked for him: the more life threw at him, the more he found solace in writing. His most successful play had been written while he was in prison, during the second year of his incarceration, after a year of not being allowed to read or write.

Angus King was a man of genius, and like many gifted minds in a particular field, he had blinders on when it came to the different ways other people besides himself might deal with life.

The first evening they arrived in Paris, in the apartment on Rue de Morny, Angus boiled over.

"Tomorrow at noon we're going to lunch with Emile de Chabanais. Do you even remember who Emile de Chabanais is?"

Elfie heaved an insolent sigh. Angus went on ingratiatingly.

"Emile de Chabanais is the man who offered to publish one of your articles in his newspaper, *Free Thought?* You haven't forgotten about the opportunity he's offered you, have you, young lady?"

"No, Angus, I haven't forgotten! But I have nothing to say. It must be true that I'm good for nothing but being a lowly alibi after all. You can go have lunch with him without me, it's as simple as that!"

Angus threw his napkin down on the table.

"I'm going out!"

Late that night, King passed by Elfie's bedroom. In the glow of the oil lamp, he saw her writing at her desk.

At breakfast, Angus asked, "So, did you finish your article?"

"No, I'm sorry, I didn't. I understand what a great opportunity Mr. de Chabanais is giving me, Angus, I assure you. But I just can't."

"Don't worry about it. Come to lunch with us anyway today. I'll surely convince Emile to wait patiently until you finish your paper. It will be better than avoiding him, and it will give you a change of scenery."

"Do you really think so?"

At the restaurant, Elfie felt out of her depth. The men talked about their stay in Italy. Mr. de Chabanais knew of the Vecchie Rovines by reputation. Then they discussed politics, a subject that Elfie did not keep up with at all. She would have had to at least read the newspapers, but Angus gave her so many books to read that she never had the time.

Finally, Angus handed a text to Emile, who skimmed it quickly. They discussed it and then Mr. de Chabanais placed it carefully next to his plate.

"And you, Miss Montesquiou, what do you have to show me?"

Elfie trembled and started to open her mouth, but remained speechless.

"Here, Emile," said Angus, handing him a page covered with writing that Elfie recognized as her own. "I have her paper right here!"

Mr. de Chabanais took the page and read it attentively. Elfie felt more humiliated than ever. She shot an angry look at Angus who must have, during the night, stolen the poem that she had composed the evening before, the only piece of writing she had managed to produce since they had left Italy.

To the Old Ruins,

To the poor libertines, enslaved by their lust,
To those ignoble lost men whose deeds stir disgust.
Abusing innocence is not a victory,
Vanquishing an honest woman brings no glory.
Seducing the pure maiden with an untrue smile,
Like a snake-charmer beguiling the trusting child,
Convinced there is art in your lecherous ways,
In decadent salons you go brag of your prey.
The innocence, the youth, so easy to betray,
Will find the strength to survive your base little ways.
Although your sordid games have reached a new low,
Your shameful attempts will surely bring you much woe.
To unscrupulous men who tell nothing but lies,
Young ladies will no longer give up their sweet sighs.
If robbing the cradle is a cowardly deed,
Sneaking away is the weak deserter's creed.
When will unwary maidens be taught to reject
The seducer who claims to guide and to instruct?
If by the fair man she agrees to be courted,
Mind you, sweet-talking fox, your ploys will be thwarted.
Dear maiden, your ignorance is no source of shame,
The immoral liars are the ones to be blamed.
Gentlemen, no battle is won in the boudoir,
Glory is earned but by real men of honor.
At the feet of the Old Ruins falls the young rake,
Entombed in the brambles, he will rot like a snake.
And maidens with flowers will drink at the fountain,
Laughing at the seducer, who looks like a chump,
Dancing on the grave of the player who deserves
No prayers from the loves he knew not how to serve.

Life Emotions

Emile de Chabanais looked at Elfie directly in the eyes.

"I am sorry that your stay in Italy was a disappointment to you, mademoiselle. But don't lose hope, all men are not cut from the same cloth."

Elfie, sitting with dignity on her chair and a polite smile on her lips, reached out her hand to take back her poem. Emile hastily pulled it away from her.

"I'm keeping it, mademoiselle. This Life Emotions speaks for all women who have been hurt by those unscrupulous seducers. I'm publishing it!"

"But… sir… you can not. The truth is that Angus stole it from me! He gave it to you without having consulted me first."

"He was right to do so. If you had come empty handed, our collaborations would have been over!"

"But I must make some changes to it."

"Why?"

"Well, for starters, the title! It clearly refers to a certain person, which is not good form."

"Yes, you're right. In this whole affair, you're the one who has not behaved properly," replied Mr. de Chabanais ironically. "Shame on you, mademoiselle."

"No, it's not that!" returned Elfie. "I mean… I don't want it to become public," she whispered.

"Who knows the secret identity of Life Emotions? In London, they are wondering who this English man is— by writing in French, you are putting them off your trail even more."

"Someone, someday, might make the connection?"

"Between a writer whose nationality is in question and a cute and naive little salon singer? You write: Robbing the cradle is a cowardly deed. Let the coward at least know what you think of him. It's well put."

"But that's just it. He will know who wrote the article, and..."

"...and will never dare," interrupted Chabanais, "brag about being called a coward and a chump by a little girl for all France to hear!"

"But..."

"My last argument in favor of publication is this, mademoiselle: your poem will arouse the curiosity of socialites who will try to ascertain the identities of the characters. Readers love puzzles, revenge, and duels in the newspapers..."

Gossipers, thought Elfie.

"... with this issue of *Free Thought?* I'll sell twice as many copies!"

She chewed her lower lip and then narrowed her green eyes, their flecks of gold starting to shine even more brilliantly.

"...Very well, but in that case, sir, my poem is worth twice the amount of the usual rate!" said Elfie triumphantly.

"You are only a beginner. I don't know if I can count on you for the long haul."

"Please give me back my paper, Mr. de Chabanais," she said serenely.

"Alright, you win this time! But we will renegotiate for the next article," he said, holding out his hand to shake on it.

Angus laughed heartily, happy to see his nightingale on the road to recovery.

"King, are you the one who planned this whole setup?"

"Absolutely not. This time, Emile, you have been manipulated by a sixteen-year-old girl."

"This is a first for me," he admitted, losing gracefully. "Let's make a toast!"

"I couldn't agree more!" enthused Angus, signaling a server to bring champagne.

Elfie was not yet on the road to recovery; she was only pretending to feel better. She said nothing about it to Angus, because she sensed that he had intentionally put some distance between them. Yet now was when she most needed to feel his strong arms around her shoulders. She hoped that Angus was just trying to be respectful, but she wasn't sure of anything anymore.

The next day, in Rue de Morny, Pierre Pastel came to personally deliver the jewelry that he had designed and made for her. It was magnificent. Elfie was moved to think that this was the first significant item she had purchased for herself with her alibi wages.

The young Pierre glowed with happiness, but the drawn features on his thin face showed that he was working a lot. Elfie worried that he wasn't eating enough. Was he earning enough to nourish himself properly? Angus, delighted to see him again, asked him to stay for dinner. Pierre didn't have to be asked twice and ate voraciously.

"I'm eating just fine, Miss Elfie, thank you for your concern. But, I don't know, I must use up more energy than I take in," he said, gladly accepting a second helping. "Thank you, it's really delicious."

It was a joy to see Pierre again. With animated enthusiasm, he recounted everything that had happened to him since he had been living in Paris. Elfie was happy for him, but she could tell that Angus and Pierre would have preferred to be alone. She sincerely thanked Pierre for his excellent work and promised to pass along more orders to him as soon as she could. She hadn't been sleeping very much or very well since they had left Italy, so she excused herself and retired to her room shortly after dinner.

As soon as they were alone, the young man expressed his concern.

"Elfie doesn't seem to be quite herself, Angus. Is something bothering her?"

Elfie, still in the corridor, slowed her pace.

"Oh, it will pass!" Angus replied. "Let's focus on us right now!"

Why did Pierre get to have the comfort of Angus's embrace, when she herself needed it so badly? Deep down, the only thing she had ever wanted was to be held in someone's loving arms. For years she had yearned for cuddles from her mother, but always in vain. Fathers didn't hug, and the nuns at boarding school, as much as they would have liked to show a bit of affection, were not allowed to. Elfie realized that, during these nine months of living with Angus, she had received more hugs from him than she ever had from anyone else in her life. And it was good for her; she loved the affection.

But on this particular evening, the alibi held back her tears and went up to bed alone.

EPISODE 15

Emotional Tailspin

It would be a long time yet before Elfie was healed. She felt betrayed, laid bare. But what's more, she felt hatred for Volpe and this black stain on her heart disturbed her. She didn't want to let herself become poisoned by resentment, which would only end up harming herself, just like Sister Fiona had taught her. Sister Fiona, who always had a smile on her face, didn't wait for life to smile on her, but always smiled first, confident that one day life would smile back.

Ever since her unfortunate experience with Volpe, Elfie distrusted all men. It was unfair, discouraging, and it wasn't what she really wanted. But it was still too soon for her to remain untroubled at the memory of her summer in Florence, or even better, to not think of it at all.

This was her state of mind when she arrived at Lord Wanton's in London, at his residence on Old Queen Street. As on their two previous stays, the Earl of Ash and Rock had a carriage waiting for them. But this time, not at Victoria Station. Angus and Elfie had taken a steamboat directly from Boulogne to London Bridge, which meant they avoided a stopover in Folkestone, since that town held bad memories for Elfie and she preferred to avoid it.

They had left Lord Wanton's last April just after Angus had found Timothy in Elfie's room, which had precipitated their departure. Ever since, the relationship between Lord Wanton and Elfie had remained unclear, and the Earl was not convinced that she hadn't come between himself and Angus.

In Saint-Julien-du-Sault and in Naples, Elfie had asked Angus if he would mind or if he considered it out of place for her to write to Lord Wanton. Since he had given his blessing, she had taken pleasure in writing him letters. But she had received nothing back from the Earl except a polite *Best regards to Miss Montesquiou* at the bottom of his letters to Angus. That had bothered her. Lord Wanton was an unusual, enigmatic man, but she liked him. Of course, he had tried to seduce her, but completely above board, with no false promises or undue pressure. Elfie felt comfortable with him. Even though he led a life in complete contradiction to the moral code that had been drilled into her since birth, she respected him.

As the carriage passed by Big Ben, Elfie's apprehension increased at the thought of seeing Lord Wanton again, but she didn't have a choice. She was paid to be King's alibi, and in London more than anywhere else, she had to be at his side. Lord Wanton had told her that once she became a woman, he would lose all interest in her. But Timothy was important to Angus.

I'll just have to be discreet and make sure I don't get in Lord Wanton's way while we're staying in his home, thought Elfie. *Angus is planning on staying for no more than a week, so I'll just stay in my rooms; it's not for very long. I'll put the time to good use by reading and writing, if I still can. This past summer, I tended to forget that I was being paid to be an alibi. This job is fulfilling enough for me— I'll simply focus on doing the job well! But I must really think of other ways to earn my keep. I can't let myself be dragged around from country to country, always holding on to Angus's hand. He is… but what is he, really, who is he, for me?*

Her reflections had caused her almond-shaped eyes to elongate toward her temples.

"Relax," Angus told her, "What's wrong with you?"

Immediately, she smiled.

"Nothing. Everything's fine."

"If you say so!"

"… I'd appreciate it if you didn't say anything about…"

"Volpe?"

"Yes."

"That's your business."

"Thank you, Angus."

"But we're talking about Timothy. All he'll need is one look at you to guess what's happened."

"You men are not all clairvoyant, you know!" grumbled Elfie. "And I'm not a little girl anymore!"

Lord Wanton welcomed them with open arms, but not to the point of coming out to greet them— he awaited them in his drawing room. Angus gave him news of his wife Graciosa; Timothy only half listened as he studied Elfie. Embarrassed, she looked away, smiling politely, pretending to be interested in what Angus was saying.

"You're not listening to me, Tim," said Angus.

"You're right, I'm not. Graciosa bores me as much as she bores you, Angus. Her only quality was beauty, and that has faded. Last winter I noticed that she had already given everything she had to give. She's an empty shell."

Even though she was no longer fond of the Countess, Elfie was shocked to hear Graciosa's husband denigrate her so rudely behind her back, but she refrained from making any comment so as not to draw attention to herself.

"Would it be alright with you," asked Angus, "if I leave you two alone until tea time? I don't know what's wrong with me, but I've been extremely tired for the last few days."

"Not at all. Get some rest, Angus. Miss Elfie and I will take a little walk in the garden while it's still nice out."

Angus shot him a severe look.

"Agreeably. On foot. Between civilized people," added Lord Wanton.

"Very well. See you two in a little while."

"Come, miss, let's take a walk in the garden. We can admire the late flowers."

"As you wish, Lord Wanton."

He took her hand under his arm and led her outside.

It was nice out. By staying under the tall plane trees, they could keep out of the sun's rays, while breathing in the fragrance of the lilies bordering the green, neatly clipped lawn. They walked for a few minutes in silence, and then Lord Wanton spoke.

"Tell me a little more, Miss Elfie, about this Pierre Pastel whom you mentioned in your letter from Saint-Julien-du-Sault. Angus said nothing about him."

"This evening, at supper, I will show you the jewelry he designed and made for me."

"So you saw him again when you stopped over in Paris?"

"Yes. But… if there is something in particular you would like to know, Lord Wanton, I'm not the right person to talk to," replied Elfie, who was uncomfortable with this interrogation.

He took the hint and changed the subject.

"So, tell me, miss, who was it that made you into a woman?"

"Ex… excuse me?"

"You don't want to tell me?"

"But, there is nothing to say, Lord Wanton," said Elfie in a low voice.

"I received the latest issue of *Free Thought?* this morning," he said, implying that he had read her poem.

It wasn't that Elfie didn't want to confide in Lord Wanton; she knew she could count on her host's discretion. But she wasn't ready yet to talk lucidly about her upsetting experience.

"Your agapanthus lilies are absolutely magnificent, Your Lordship. I've never seen such blue ones before."

"Thank you for your letters," he replied, as if she hadn't tried to change the subject. "There weren't very many of them, but I enjoyed them."

"There weren't very many?" Elfie couldn't help but retort, trying to keep her voice lighthearted. "What about all the ones you didn't write to me?"

"That was a test. To see if you cared whether or not you heard from me," he said with a smile, caressing his blond mustache. "I see that it meant something to you. Your poem wasn't too bad. A bit too conventional for my tastes, and Chabanais's tastes too, I imagine, but he's more concerned with the number of copies he sells than the quality of the writing."

"I completely agree."

"Why did you sell it to him then?"

"For very down-to-earth reasons that you wouldn't understand, Lord Wanton."

"Your tongue is quite sharp, miss. Let's go back to the one subject that interests me."

Elfie removed her arm from Timothy's. Irritated that he wanted to talk about Volpe again, she replied curtly.

"Why are you asking me, when you already know, since you've read my poem? So that you can chide me with *I warned you, little page!* Or perhaps point out to me that if I had continued with your *lessons*, then I would have known how to protect myself better? And let's talk about your lessons, Lord Wanton! Weren't you the one who opened the door to..."

"You're mixing everything up, Miss Elfie..."

"Don't tell me what to think, Lord Wanton! Wouldn't you have taken advantage of my... body, too, if I had let you? What's the difference, in the end?"

"The difference is that, while I indeed love your divine form, miss, I love what's on the inside just as much. I could not love a person solely for their beauty. I think that the soul and the mind are indivisible from the body. I take great pleasure in admiring your gentle curves and I would take even greater pleasure in caressing them. Yet I don't consider your mind to be superfluous. But obviously that fact has escaped you. Perhaps your mind is not what I thought it was, or haven't you been listening..."

"If I keep listening to you, Lord Wanton, I'm going to hear you scold me with something like, *I told you so!*"

"No, you won't. That's not my style," he replied, surprised by her vehemence.

"That's right. Your style is to give out lessons, without even being able to set foot in a boat to travel with your friend Angus, which would have given you the opportunity to know exactly what his relationship with Mr. Pastel is, instead of questioning me about it!"

Even as these biting words left her mouth, Elfie realized that she had gone too far. Lord Wanton had put up with more from Elfie in the last five minutes than he had tolerated from anyone since his childhood. He stiffened and shot her a malevolent look with his two different-colored eyes.

"Please excuse me, Lord Wanton. I spoke without thinking. I'm sorry."

But he turned on his heels and went back to the house without another word, leaving her alone in the garden. Elfie had the horrible sensation that the earth was opening up under her feet. Distraught, she collapsed onto a little wooden bench behind her. Who was she to dare speak like that to a man in Lord Wanton's position? A pathetic adventuress who made a living by throwing herself into the arms of the man who paid her whenever a police officer appeared? She would be fired from her job, if it ever was a job. Lord Wanton was right, her articles were not the best ever written and who knows if their only interest was in the fact that she was the great Angus King's companion? She would be thrown out into the streets, and that terrified her.

A wave of rage swept over her as she thought of Volpe. He had stealthily wrapped himself around her heart like the thousands of tiny barbs on the golden hops vines that were climbing and twining their way up the little arbor against the wall behind her. Volpe had injected her heart with a venom as poisonous as the arum lilies flowering in the middle of the lawn. Again, she was beset with thoughts of bloody revenge, and she fought to hold back the furious scream that rose up from within her. She took deep breaths of the perfumed air that already held a hint of late-afternoon humidity from the garden and stood up. She had to tell Angus about her conversation with Lord Wanton. Either he would calm Timothy down, or he would get angry and kick her out, but at least she would know. That was better than agonizing about it alone in the garden.

As she climbed the magnificent staircase of polished brown wood, Elfie wondered how to present things to Angus. Should she be humble and submissive? Vindictive? Hurt? For the first time, she went into Angus's rooms without knocking; always before, whenever they had shared the same room in a hotel or inn, she had been careful to ask before entering, unlike Angus, who just barged in.

In the doorway, she looked up and saw Angus near the bed, facing her and, from the back, Lord Wanton wearing no shirt. Lord Wanton's back was covered with nasty-looking scars made long ago by a whip or a stick. Surprised by this horrific sight, Elfie let out a startled cry. Lord Wanton turned around and looked at her spitefully. She quickly backed out into the hallway, exclaiming, "I'm sorry, I'm sorry!"

She ran to her room, but not before she heard Lord Wanton hiss to Angus, "That's it, she no longer amuses me.

You can send her away!"

End of Season 3
To be continued,

ELFIE, Season 4
In this Season 3, Elfie got hurt. With a heavy heart still seething with rage, she will follow Angus to America where new adventures await them…

NOTES BY GABRIELLE DUBOIS:

About the TRAVELING JOURNEYMEN (Compagnons du Devoir)

The traveling journeymen in Saint-Julien-du-Sault were members of the Compagnons du Devoir Association. This group consisted of young men in training to become carpenters, furniture makers, bricklayers, stonemasons, etc. They would leave their hometowns and their first workshops in order to gain experience, learn new techniques, and work in various settings with masters of their crafts. This tour through France was also a gradual rite of initiation into an elite line of work. There were different stages of hierarchy, rules that the members followed, and rituals and special vocabulary that united them as a group while at the same time setting them apart from average workers.

At the beginning of the century, these journeymen traveled by foot or sometimes in horse-drawn carts, even after the advent of the train. Although this journey was often made alone, the arrival of a compagnon in town proved the strength of the ties that united these journeymen in a shared sense of duty and devotion to their craft and to each other: besides food and shelter, the local point man, or rouleur, had to find him a job or send him to a fellow compagnon in another town who would give him a job as apprentice. These workers acquired a wider experience than the average laborers of that time period, thanks to this deliberate yet fluid mobility.

The Bons Enfants Inn in Saint-Julien-du-Sault, which still exists as a hotel today, was an inn that hosted these traveling journeymen on their tour of France in the

19th century. Although the name of the inn means "good children," these journeymen were not always so good, sometimes assaulting the young women in the regions they passed through. Each line of work had its own rules and the compagnons showed their pride in belonging to one craft or another by facing off and fighting each other with the tools of their trade: hammers, compasses, knives, etc....

About ITALY:

Sexual Tourism:
In the 19th century, a trip to Italy was considered the culmination of every young, wealthy Englishman's education. But besides the culture (paintings, sculptures, churches, museums, etc...) many young (and not so young) men took trips to Italy for another reason. Since homosexuality was outlawed in the United Kingdom, they found male prostitutes in Italy, in Naples in particular, and could travel with a male companion without fearing prison.

Music and Singing:
The great songs of the opera were commonly sung in the streets, in families, among friends, by the populace in general.

Tourist Boats:
The hotel porters swarming out to meet Elfie and Angus's boat was a common occurrence. The same sort of scene played out when arriving in Spain by boat, at Cadiz or Malaga. French poet Théophile Gautier describes such a scene in his book Voyage to Spain: "To get to shore, they had to transport us and our effects in little dinghies whose owners fought over the travelers and the trunks with

wild vociferations, similar to the *coucou* carriage drivers in Paris heading off to Montmorency or Vincennes. It was exceedingly difficult to avoid getting separated from my comrade, for we were pulled to the left by one, while another one tugged us to the right with unsettling force, especially if you remember that these squabbles were taking place on little rowboats that the least movement might tip over like a swing under the feet of the struggling crowd." Likewise, when you disembarked onto the docks of the Seine River near Paris, the *coucou* drivers nearly assaulted you (the *coucous* were the public horse-drawn carriages that provided transportation to the suburbs of Paris). They eventually disappeared, replaced by horse-drawn omnibuses and then by the train.

The SONGS

The song *Mme Arthur* written by Paul de Kock in the 1850s was still sung in the 1930s by the famous Yvette Guilbert:

Madame Arthur est une femme
Qui fit parler, parler, parler, parler d'elle longtemps,
Sans journaux, sans rien, sans réclame
Elle eut une foule d'amants,
Chacun voulait être aimé d'elle,
Chacun la courtisait, pourquoi?
C'est que sans être vraiment belle,
Elle avait un je ne sais quoi!

Madame Arthur est une femme
Qui fit parler, parler, parler, parler d'elle longtemps,
Sans journaux, sans rien, sans réclame
Elle eut une foule d'amants,
Madame Arthur est une femme

Qui fit parler d'elle longtemps.

Sa taille était très ordinaire,
Ses yeux petits [ter] mais sémillants,
Son nez retroussé, sa voix claire,
Ses pieds cambrés et frétillants
Bref, en regardant sa figure,
Rien ne vous donnait de l'émoi;
Mais par derrière sa tournure
Promettait un je ne sais quoi!

Madame Arthur est une femme
Qui fit parler, parler, parler, parler d'elle longtemps,
Sans journaux, sans rien, sans réclame
Elle eut une foule d'amants,
Madame Arthur est une femme
Qui fit parler d'elle longtemps.

Ses amants lui restaient fidèles,
C'est elle qui les renvoyait
Elle aimait les ardeurs nouvelles,
Un vieil amour lui déplaisait
Et chacun, le chagrin dans l'âme,
De son cœur n'ayant plus l'emploi,
Disait : hélas ! une autre femme
N'aura pas son je ne sais quoi !
Il fallait la voir à la danse ;
Son entrain était sans égal
Par ses mouvements, sa prestance,
Elle était la Reine du bal
Au cavalier lui faisant face
Son pied touchait le nez, ma foi,
Chacun applaudissait sa grâce
Et surtout son je ne sais quoi!

De quoi donc vivait cette dame?
Montrant un grand train de maison,
Courant au vaudeville, au drame,
Rien qu'à l'avant-scène dit-on
Elle voyait pour l'ordinaire
Venir son terme sans effroi,
Car alors son propriétaire
Admirait son je ne sais quoi!

Oh ! femme qui cherchez à faire
Des conquêtes matin et soir,
En vain vous passez pour vous plaire
Des heures à votre miroir,
Élégance, grâce mutine,
Regard, soupir de bon aloi,
Velours, parfums et crinoline,
Rien ne vaut un je ne sais quoi!

The song *Sidonie* written by Paul de Kock in the 1850s was still sung in the 1960s by Brigitte Bardot:

Sidonie a plus d'un amant,
C'est une chose bien connue
Qu'elle avoue, elle, fièrement,
Sidonie a plus d'un amant.

Parce que pour elle, être nue
Est son plus charmant vêtement.
C'est une chose bien connue,
Sidonie a plus d'un amant.

Elle en prend à ses cheveux blonds
Comme à sa toile l'araignée
Prend les mouches et les frelons,
Elle en prend à ses cheveux blonds.

Vers sa prunelle ensoleillée
Ils volent, pauvres papillons.
Comme à sa toile l'araignée,
Elle en prend à ses cheveux blonds.

Elle les mène par le nez,
Comme fait, dit-on, le crotale,
Des oiseaux qu'il a fascinés.
Elle les mène par le nez.

Quand dans une moue elle étale
Sa langue à leurs yeux étonnés,
Comme fait, dit-on, le crotale,
Elle les mène par le nez.

Elle en attrape avec les dents
Quand le rire entrouvre sa bouche,
Et dévore les imprudents.
Elle en attrape avec les dents.

Sa bouche, quand elle se couche,
Reste rose et ses dents dedans
Quand le rire entrouvre sa bouche,
Elle en attrape avec les dents.

Sidonie a plus d'un amant,
Qu'on le lui reproche ou l'en loue,
Elle s'en moque également,
Sidonie a plus d'un amant.

Aussi jusqu'à ce qu'on la cloue
Au sapin de l'enterrement,
Qu'on le lui reproche ou l'en loue,
Sidonie aura plus d'un amant.

The song *Plaisir d'Amour* written by Jean-Pierre Claris

de Florian, music by Jean-Paul Égide Martini, in 1784 was sung by many French singers until the late 20th century, but also by Joan Baez and Marianne Faithfull:

> Plaisir d'amour ne dure qu'un moment,
> Chagrin d'amour dure toute la vie.
>
> J'ai tout quitté pour l'ingrate Sylvie,
> Elle me quitte et prend un autre amant.
> Plaisir d'amour ne dure qu'un moment,
> Chagrin d'amour dure toute la vie.
>
> Tant que cette eau coulera doucement
> Vers ce ruisseau qui borde la prairie,
> Je t'aimerai, me répétait Sylvie;
> L'eau coule encor, elle a changé pourtant!
>
> Plaisir d'amour ne dure qu'un moment,
> Chagrin d'amour dure toute la vie.

The very popular song *À la claire fontaine* was written between the 15 and 18th century.in France or in Québec, or in between by a traveler?

> À la claire fontaine
> M'en allant promener
> J'ai trouvé l'eau si belle
> Que je m'y suis baignée
> Il y a longtemps que je t'aime jamais je ne t'oublierai
>
> Sous les feuilles d'un chêne
> Je me suis fait sécher
> Sur la plus haute branche
> Un rossignol chantait
> Il y a longtemps que je t'aime jamais je ne t'oublierai

Chante, rossignol, chante
Toi qui as le cœur gai
Tu as le cœur à rire
Moi, je l'ai à pleurer
Il y a longtemps que je t'aime jamais je ne t'oublierai

J'ai perdu mon ami
Sans l'avoir mérité
Pour un bouton de rose
Que j'ai trop tôt donné
Il y a longtemps que je t'aime jamais je ne t'oublierai

Je voudrais que la rose
Fût encore au rosier
Et que mon ami Pierre
Fût encore à m'aimer
Il y a longtemps que je t'aime jamais je ne t'oublierai

ABOUT MARYBETH TIMMERMANN
the TRANSLATOR:

Marybeth Timmermann is an ATA-certified French to English translator specializing in literature, academic writing, certified documents, and revision/proofreading. In addition to translating fiction, she is a longtime contributing translator and editor to  *The Beauvoir Series*, a seven-volume collection of the writings of French author, philosopher, and feminist Simone de Beauvoir, published in English translation by the University of Illinois Press.

www.timmermanntranslations.com

ABOUT GABRIELLE DUBOIS
the AUTHOR:

 Gabrielle Dubois is a French author and novelist who specializes in 19th century history. She is a champion of women everywhere and Founding General Partner of The 51 Fund, which funds the production of films written and directed by women. Her historical series LOUISE 1 'Mistress Mine' and LOUISE 2 'Where are you roaming' are already published in English. Her other novels CALIXTE and VIOLETTE are available in French.
https://www.gabrielle-dubois.com/
Instagram @gabrielleduboisauthor

See you in ELFIE Season 4!

From a summer in Italy to a winter in America. This new world, so far from their age-old Europe, turns out to be charming and exhilarating. Surrounded by so much hard-working, youthful energy and hope, it's easy to believe that anything is possible in this young nation on the cusp of a new era following their recent Civil War. But the freedom newly granted to the former slaves is still far from liberating a people, far from accepting a man such as Angus, and even farther from liberating women, whether they are Black or white. Elfie experiences this painful reality first hand. In this fourth season of ELFIE, we see, through the eyes of Elfie, how French people saw Americans in the 19th century, thanks to the meticulous, behind-the-scenes research of author Gabrielle Dubois. It's humorous, serious, interesting, and always fascinating, with illustrations for each chapter that immerse us into the book as if we were watching a movie.